LOVE: A STORY

Love: A Story

A novel

by

BILL SMOOT

BOOKS

Adelaide Books
New York / Lisbon
2019

LOVE: A STORY
A novel
By Bill Smoot
Copyright © by Bill Smoot
Cover design © 2019 Adelaide Books

Published by Adelaide Books, New York / Lisbon
adelaidebooks.org

Editor-in-Chief
Stevan V. Nikolic

For any information, please address Adelaide Books
at info@adelaidebooks.org

or write to:

Adelaide Books
244 Fifth Ave. Suite D27
New York, NY, 10001

ISBN-10: 1-950437-81-7
ISBN-13: 978-1-950437-81-8

Printed in the United States of America

This book is dedicated with great admiration and respect to

my students past and present

in the Prison University Project at San Quentin.

Contents

PART ONE: LOVE HAPPENS

1

Could it be?

It was!—a stroller, rolling down shady, winding Euclid Avenue, gathering speed in the oncoming lane. Michael hit the brakes, jerked the car into park, flung open the door, and jumped out just in time to grab the stroller by its handle and pull it to a gentle stop. The canopy had fallen forward. Expecting the face of a terrified toddler, he pushed the canopy back. The seat was empty.

He looked up the street and saw the mother on the sidewalk, baby in her arms, waving. After turning on his emergency flashers and closing the car door, he pushed the empty stroller back up the hill. He could see from the swiveling double front wheels how it had been stable enough not to turn over. His heart was still pounding.

Embarrassed and flustered, the mother thanked him and apologized. He waved off the apology with a joke about the Odessa steps. She got the reference. This was Berkeley.

Driving up the hill, he turned off the radio to let the event soak in. His wife Leanna had decided recently that she was ready to have a baby. The runaway stroller was his call to fatherhood. His leaping out to save the baby meant he was ready. It was a momentous sign in the story of his life.

Lives *are* stories, aren't they? We say, "Tell me the story of your life." Or, "That's the story of my life."

But what makes a story? Not events. Suppose we followed a person for even a single day and recorded every act, every time he touched his earlobe or took another step walking to lunch. Suppose we recorded every perception and every half-thought (imagine thought-recognition software wired to his brain). A single day would fill a thousand pages. A person's life, ten million pages!

When we ask for the story of someone's life, we don't want it all. A story is selective. It is the moments that matter. It is the soul-glue that holds those moments together. It is their meaning. That is why the storyteller uses poetic devices.

In Michael's story, the stroller was a symbol, a foreshadowing of fatherhood. To invoke Chekhov's famous example, it was the gun on the wall in act one, bound to be fired before the end of the play.

2

Michael had met Leanna five years earlier, when she was twenty-five and he was thirty-nine, making her just shy of the French formula of half his age plus seven. She was a graduate student in chemistry at Berkeley, modeling on the side, and he hired her as a nude model for a photo shoot. He taught English at a prep school across the bay in Marin County, and photography was an avocation. His love was black and white, nudes and still-lifes mostly, and he had shot enough summer weddings to pay for his equipment. A guest cottage behind his house doubled as a photography studio, its tiny kitchen serving as a darkroom.

Their first session produced the best image he had ever made. Shot in a darkened studio and rim-lit from behind, the image was a nude in dark silhouette, s-curved lines surrounded by a nimbus of silver light.

When Leanna had first stepped out of her robe, he thought her body too boyish: thin, with tiny breasts and a flat behind. He privately doubted he would end up with any images he could use, but he would never communicate this to a model.

But he was wrong. She understood that posing was stop-action dance. She knew how to make her body transcend itself, as a good actor becomes a character. By the end of the shoot, he was hopeful. When, in the red glow of his darkroom, he watched the image rise in the tray of developer, he was stunned by its beauty. He printed some 16x20s, and a month later one of the prints won acceptance into a national photography exhibit, his greatest success yet.

In celebration, he asked Leanna to do another modeling session, and afterwards they went out for Indian food. It was a fun dinner. At the beginning of his summer vacation, she emailed asking if she could stay for a week in the studio-cottage behind his house. She offered to pay some rent. She needed a break from her apartment mates, one of whom had just graduated and was keeping Leanna awake with loud out-of-town visitors. Michael wasn't in the mood to entertain a guest, especially during the first week of his summer break, and he didn't feel right taking rent money from her, but after clarifying that she would be more a tenant on her own than his guest, he said okay.

When she arrived on a Saturday morning, he handed her the key to the cottage and then drove off to photograph a wedding in San Francisco. The next day they went for a run together, and on a whim he invited her to dinner. He had to cook anyway, so why not? He made pasta with summer vegetables and pesto chicken sausage, and a salad of baby lettuces, black mission figs, and baked goat cheese. For dessert he had bought raspberry sorbet and tiny chocolate truffles. Freed from his position behind the camera (working with models, he was always the paradigm of professional respect and artistic detachment), he found her cute, charming, personable, and sexy. Too bad she was so young. He wished he would meet someone like her but ten years older. After dinner, they drank tea on his deck then she retired to the cottage.

The next day when she returned from a modeling gig (she was taking the week off from the lab), he was working in his garden. She offered to take him to dinner with her modeling money—a thank you for letting her stay the week—and they ate at a Thai restaurant in Berkeley. He found it a sweet gesture. She told him about her research project and her frustrations in the chemistry PhD program. It drove her crazy that any idea took six months of tedious work to test. The next day she had no modeling job, so they drove out to Muir Beach, put on their jackets, and took a long hike along the foggy coast. She had stopped at the farmer's market and packed them a picnic lunch.

As they hiked, he pointed out names of coastal flowers, tracks in the dust left by snakes, the sign that warned of mountain lions. She told him about growing up half in Singapore and half in Texas. Beneath her matter-of-fact account he sensed an unspoken sadness, an edge of anger. Nothing bonds us to others quite like hearing their stories, and Leanna's touched his heart. When she asked about a particular restaurant in San Francisco she had read about, he spontaneously offered to take her as his guest.

That evening, after they had ordered cocktails, she looked around with appreciation and awe. She said that it was the nicest restaurant she had ever been in. Then she looked at him and said, "I'm so happy I could cry."

Her words pierced his heart.

We are all familiar with the kitchy Valentine's Day Cupid, a rosy-cheeked, winged cherub with arrows and quiver, pop culture metaphor for piercing the heart. But as Michael and Leanna sipped their drinks—hers a cocktail of pomegranate juice and vodka, his a Manhattan—there was no third power, no cherubic god of love, with a bow. Leanna, not Cupid, shot the arrow—without knowledge or intention, of course (the most dangerous kind of arrow). The arrow said, "You have just made me happy." It implied, "You have the power to make me happy. I am open to you in that way." If each of us is a fortified castle, she had just raised her portcullis and invited him in.

3

What had brought Leanna to this moment of the pomegranate cocktail?

She was born in Singapore. Her mother was a nurse, her father a good-natured ne'er-do-well who spent evenings gambling with his buddies, leaving the two children to their mother. When Leanna was six, Ma divorced Pa and moved to Texas with Leanna and her younger brother to marry an older Chinese-American businessman who had fallen in love with her on his business trips to Singapore. In Texas, "Uncle," as Leanna would always call him, proved to be an attentive father and husband. Though he turned out to be not as financially well-off as Ma had been led to believe, he provided adequately for the family, he did not drink or gamble, and he was devoted to Ma and her two children.

The dominant metaphor in Ma's life story was a ladder. She believed that the goal of living was to climb, rung by rung, the higher the better. To her, life in Texas with Uncle was a rung or two higher than her life in Singapore with Pa.

She tried to instill climbing skills in her children. When they arrived in America, she taught Leanna and her brother to use a knife and fork instead of chopsticks. She taught them not to pick their noses in public as they had in Singapore. They must pronounce their words like Americans and not speak "Singlish." They should work hard in school and learn to play a musical instrument. They should attend the Christian Church for the future doors that might open—not in heaven but on earth. Ma was not a spiritual person.

By the time Leanna reached junior high, she felt a little dizzy on the ladder. As the only Asian kid in her grade, she was viewed by her classmates as a skinny, slant-eyed nerd with big glasses, a stick-like body and a flat chest (was she just a boy in disguise?), who only studied, played her clarinet, and got top grades. The boys teased her by sticking their faces in hers and pulling their eyelids to the side. They called her Larry instead of Leanna. To the blond girls with lengthening legs and swelling breasts, she was invisible. When the boys laughed that she should not be using the girls' restroom, she tightened her jaw and walked fast. Something inside of her hardened, like the tip of an iron spear.

Their house beyond the outer suburbs of Dallas was a one-story concrete block structure built in stages by the least expensive subcontractors Uncle could find. The lot that Uncle had purchased for cheap was located between some small farms where people had horses and chickens and a rough neighborhood where people sold drugs and kept pit bulls. Ma would not let them get a dog, but they had chickens. Chickens earned their keep by laying eggs.

Ma came to doubt that the local high school would help Leanna climb to a higher rung. So when the family visited Singapore the summer after Leanna finished eighth grade, Ma announced that Leanna would stay in Singapore for high school and live with Pa, who had an apartment and a steady job driving a cab. Leanna felt like a ping-pong ball batted across the ocean by Ma's paddle. She also felt, in the deepest part of her heart, that Ma was abandoning her, leaving her like a skinny kitten on Pa's doorstep. She would miss her brother, Ma, and Uncle. She would not miss the kids who either teased her or made her feel invisible.

Though the ache of being abandoned lodged deep in Leanna's heart, high school in Singapore was better. They were all nerds there, Leanna less than most because she was now the girl who had lived in America. Though she was still flat chested (why won't they grow? she wondered), she now had friends and boyfriends. Here, studying hard made her respected, not teased. Here, she felt seen and heard. When she graduated four years later, she returned to Ma, her brother, and Uncle, and a year later she enrolled in a small college in Texas that Uncle decided was a good fit for her. The ping-pong ball had been batted across the ocean again.

Soon Ma became the ping-pong ball, for during Leanna's first year in college, Ma and Leanna's brother were deported for having overstayed their visas. Leanna's high school years in Singapore saved her from the same fate, and her own application for a green card—she had been legally adopted by Uncle some years before—was working its way through the bureaucracy.

By her junior year in college Leanna had found a new identity as the star student of the chemistry department, studying hard and working long hours in the lab. The darling of her professors, she won grants for summer lab work and was listed as a coauthor on a paper produced by one of her professors.

College never matched her high school years for an active social life, and the college boys she had crushes on took little notice. When she looked at herself in the mirror at twenty-two, she was not happy with what she saw—someone who looked sixteen, flat-chested but now a little chubby, with acne-prone skin, and still those glasses.

Her green card arrived just in time for her to accept a fellowship for graduate school in chemistry at Berkeley. Over that summer, she found her own ladder to climb. She changed her diet and counted calories. She worked out in the gym seven days a week, sometimes twice a day. If she gave in and ate something off her diet, she made herself throw it up. She experimented with skin products until her complexion began to clear. She got fitted for contact lenses. She worked her way up to a daily run of five miles, sometimes as much as eight. With a slimmer torso, her A-cup boobs looked more shapely, and she ordered an herbal supplement to make them grow. Her boobs did not grow, but her body became nicely toned and as sleek as a seal. She learned about fashion and make-up, and she bought herself sexy lingerie. On the treadmill, she imagined the faces of her middle school tormentors beneath her pounding feet, her sweat dripping into their eyes.

During her first spring at Berkeley, she became lovers with a graduate student in biochemistry whose appreciation of her new body made her feel womanly and desirable. When, as gently as he could, he dumped her two months later, she fell into a dark abyss. She cried and shook, unable to eat or sleep. She could not read a page of her textbooks or hear what was said in lectures. She had never felt so lost and alone. She feared becoming invisible again. She wondered if she had the courage to take some arsenic from the lab to poison first him and then herself.

After a few very dark weeks, she clenched her fists and willed herself not to remember. She vowed to let others appreciate the body that he had passed up. She resumed exercising. She practiced in front of a mirror the poses of models in fashion magazines and in artistic nude photography books. She joined an internet site for models and photographers, and she began to do photo-shoots—fashion, lingerie, artistic nudes—first in exchange for prints and then for money. She put together a portfolio book that established her as the opposite of invisible. She had a brief affair with one of the photographers.

Now, two years later, she was sipping a pomegranate cocktail in a beautiful San Francisco restaurant with a well-dressed, well-spoken, blue-eyed Caucasian gentleman who seemed to know his way around, and suddenly she felt so happy she could cry.

4

And what had brought Michael to this moment, watching Leanna sip her pomegranate cocktail and having his heart pierced when she proclaimed that she was so happy she could cry?

He had grown up in Indiana, the only child to two loving parents, his father a dairy farmer and his mother a Latin teacher at the high school. During a boyhood out of a Norman Rockwell painting, he helped his father in the fields, attended 4-H club meetings, made the high school baseball team as a shortstop, earned good grades, and went off to college at Indiana University.

College was at first a challenge. He did not know anyone. No one knew him. He sat in lecture halls with more students than had attended his high school. The dorm food was terrible. He kept his promise to himself not to go home on the weekends. He tried out for the baseball team as a walk-on and did not make it, but he did get noticed by the coach who told him, "You're solid. If you really want to play, transfer to a division three college. You could be in the starting line-up." Michael gave himself a semester to decide, but the decision was not as much about baseball as about doubting he really belonged at IU. He felt like someone standing on a platform unsure which train he should take.

His dormitory roommate talked him into going through fraternity rush. He liked the guys at one of the houses and they invited him to join. Now he had a train to board. He felt more at home. The food was better. He learned that the secret to belonging was believing he belonged.

Then something new happened. He took a course on the American novel, and it drew him in. Seeds that had been lying dormant in his mind began to sprout. Classes began to interest him in a way that high school never had. He was awestruck by the immense world he discovered in books, and what awed him most were stories. There were stories in histories, in novels, in poems and plays, in paintings, in philosophies, in theories. He felt a greater passion for learning than he had ever felt for playing baseball.

He doubled-majored in English and philosophy, applying his farm boy work ethic to his studies. He made friends with others in his classes and gradually drifted away from his fraternity. During the Friday afternoon keggers, Michael went to a coffee house and read. During his senior year, he shared a small house with some other English majors. He stayed for a Master's Degree in English, and for the first year shared an apartment with his girlfriend, a French major. He loved her as much as he was capable as a boy of twenty-two. Then she left to study in Paris and he lived alone for the second year, writing his masters thesis and tasting for the first time solitude, a bittersweet way of being that combined a wistful loneliness with an intensity of experience. Literature had never seemed so vital.

After finishing his degree, he wandered for a few years. The change from small town boy to pensive young man left him adrift. He spent a restless summer helping his father on the farm. He waited tables in New York, where he did some freelance writing, trying now to create stories, and he learned photography. He gave up trying to write and became a serious photographer. Maybe he was meant to record stories, not create them. He drank deeply of what he saw: old people on benches, children playing by themselves, the moon reflected in a river. He tried to make it as a documentary photographer, traveling to strip mines in Kentucky, toxic dump sites in New Jersey, abandoned factories in Detroit, rusting steel mills in Pennsylvania. Though some of his work was published in photography periodicals or accepted to exhibits, he couldn't make enough money to feed himself. He assembled a portfolio of his best work and tried some galleries. The verdict seemed to be that while his work was very good, it had been done before. It was not cutting edge. The failure tasted metallic on his tongue.

Encouraged by an old graduate school classmate, he moved to the Bay Area when he was twenty-eight to take a prep school teaching job, and there he found his calling as a humanities teacher. Teaching came naturally to him; he was clear, he listened to students carefully, and by trial and error he discovered how best to engage their minds and souls with literature. His love for stories increased by teaching them. Within a few years he had earned a reputation as one of the school's best teachers. The death of his father and the sale of the farm enabled him to buy a brown shingle house in Berkeley.

His first year in Berkeley he fell in love, deeply this time, for he was a man now, and he believed he had found happiness, but it ended. Two years later he found love again, but again it was followed by heartbreak, and again the loneliness and the longing grew. He would always remember being back in Indiana for his thirty-fifth birthday, his mother dying of cancer yet rallying to bake him a birthday cake. As he blew out the candles, he made a wish that he would become a husband and a father. Now he was thirty-nine, and he was watching a twenty-five year-old sip a pomegranate cocktail while her happiness pierced his heart.

5

Leanna decided to extend her vacation in his backyard cottage for another week (somehow an email to her lab director made this possible), and Michael found himself an enthusiastic tour guide. Leanna had not explored the Bay Area much beyond the Berkeley campus, so he took her to neighborhoods in San Francisco, to new hiking trails, to the beach, to restaurants. She was a knowledgeable food lover, and one day she asked to use his kitchen to cook him a Chinese meal. When he opened the front door after a tennis game that afternoon, he smelled delicious exotic flavors wafting from the kitchen. "Honey, I'm home," he called, and after a silent pause, her laughter filled the house.

The next afternoon she was sitting on the deck in the fog with her laptop, checking her email. He brought her a cup of white tea, and as she took it, she said, "You really take care of me." The cup of tea was an arrow that pierced her heart. The cup of tea said that this was a man with the desire and the ability to care for her. Being cared for was a deeply buried desire. It was a soft target for an arrow.

In the next few days he delighted her, made her laugh, showed her new sights. They had serious talks about her work in the lab, her resentment toward her mother for playing ping-pong with Leanna's life, and her growing ambivalence about doing chemistry. One afternoon in San Francisco, they crammed themselves onto a packed cable car, and as the car lurched forward, the back of her head pressed against his face. Inhaling the smell of her hair, he told her, "I like the way your hair smells."

"It's my shampoo," she said. "Lavender."

"I can smell that, too," he said. "But the smell I like is your hair."

He realized that he had a full-blown crush on her.

He told his friend Frank about it after their tennis game the next afternoon. After listening to the story, Frank said, "So a puppy wandered into your yard, you made its tail wag, and now you've fallen in love with it"

"Love? I'm calling it a crush," Michael laughed. "Is it as crazy as you make it sound?"

Frank shrugged. "When was there ever a love that wasn't crazy?"

"Crush," Michael corrected. "Crazy crush."

Frank answered, "*Crush* is the acorn. *Love* is the oak tree. Same essence, different stage of development."

That night at dinner (again they found themselves in a nice restaurant, his treat), Michael said to her, "So what do we have here? I mean, we've been spending entire days together."

In the talk that followed, she made it clear that her feelings were Platonic, and he admitted that his had crept beyond that. Though he felt disappointed, a minor bruise to his ego would heal soon enough. Besides, she was too young for him, so this was for the best. Maybe he had found a new friend. Maybe she would introduce him to one of her single female professors.

It was true that the cup of white tea had pierced her heart, but not to the point of love. She had already composed a job description for her next lover, and this man, nice as he was, exceeded her desired age range by ten years.

The next day they went for a run together on the fire trail that wound its way into the hills behind the Berkeley campus. He felt he was slowing her pace, so half way up, he told her that she could run ahead—he wouldn't mind—since she was clearly the faster runner. As he fell behind, he looked with the discerning eye of a photographer and the appreciative gaze of a man at her tanned sleek runner's thighs and her tight butt. A couple of miles later, just where the trail flattened out, he found her stopped, bent over at the waist, her hands on her knees. "We're like the tortoise and the hare," he puffed. She fell in beside him, and they ran side by side in silence. By the time they had reached the end and turned around, he noticed her set jaw, her fixed eyes, so he asked whether something was wrong.

"I don't like to be a quitter," she said, spitting the word *quitter* in a quaking voice. He was taken aback. After all, she had never run this steep trail and could not know how to pace herself. Besides, it was a casual afternoon run, not as if they were trying out for the Olympics. When they reached the parking lot, she was brushing away hot tears of anger. They drove back to the house in silence, and she hid out in the cottage for the rest of the afternoon and evening.

Not only is she too young for me, he thought, but she's crazy besides.

Her second week in the cottage was drawing to a close, and in two days she would return to her own apartment and resume her work at the lab. Michael sat at his desk, arranging the books he had gathered for summer reading. In his desk drawer there had been languishing for three years a Christmas gift from a student's parents, a certificate for dinner at one of San Francisco's best restaurants. He had been saving it for a special occasion that had yet to occur. The incident on the running trail had cured him of his crush, but what the hell, he thought, it can be a farewell dinner. He called and made a reservation for the next night.

After they were seated in the elegant dining room, Leanna nervously told him that she felt like the country mouse visiting the city mouse, insecure and out of her element. Her simple, honest admission reactivated his crush. He told her she fit in quite nicely, and that besides, she was the most gorgeous woman there. "You're the queen mouse," he said. "You transcend city and country." Behind their table was a mirrored wall, and he told her that furthermore, she was beautiful from two directions at once. She laughed and blushed.

The waiters were as welcoming and warm as if Michael and Leanna were regulars, and from the *amuse bouche* of tomato gazpacho to the chocolate soufflé dessert, each dish tasted like an exquisite celebration in the mouth. Each course was paired with a wine like the sections of an orchestra, and the elements flowed like the movements in a symphony. With every course Leanna felt more at home in this new world. If his serving her a cup of tea had pierced her heart, that arrow in her heart was now vibrating like the strings of a cello. She was being cared for like never before. The arrow in his heart, too, was quivering, because he was making her so happy she could cry.

Back at home, feeling sated and drowsy from the food and wine, Michael went to bed. The backdoor opened, and he heard her making a cup of tea in his kitchen. He was nearly asleep when she plopped down beside him in the dark. He felt strands of her hair fall onto his face just before she placed on his mouth the most soul-shaking kiss of his life.

He caught his breath and said, "Could I have another one of those?" She laughed, and then she obliged. This was the second arrow to pierce his heart.

6

We have said that the myth of Cupid is not entirely accurate as a description of love. First, the arrow is shot not by Cupid, but by a man or woman—in this case, by Leanna. Second, the myth omits the critical detail that attached to the arrow is a cord, like the rope on a whaler's harpoon, which tethers the heart of the person shot to the shooter. The two arrows that pierced Michael's heart—making Leanna so happy she could cry on the evening of the pomegranate cocktail and now the soul-shaking kiss—bound him to her with two golden cords.

His heart having been pierced by two arrows, could he choose not to love her?

No.

Following his years of loneliness and longing, two was the magic number for heart-piercing arrows. He could resist the first arrow—and he had. It had produced a mere crush—an acorn, as Frank said. With the second, the acorn had become an oak tree. Even in love, could he choose not to continue this newborn relationship with her? Could he walk away from the oak tree? Possibly. That returns us to the issue of story.

Michael's road to watching the twenty-five year old Leanna sip a pomegranate cocktail and two weeks later receiving from her a soul-shattering kiss had been long and circuitous. Soon after moving to the Bay Area, Michael had fallen for Elizabeth, a young biology professor at Berkeley who had won him with her beauty, her statuesque body, her ability to name all of the plants on any hike they took, and her sensual, languorous manner. He was certain that she was "the one."

After a year, she abruptly fell out of love with him. A month later she changed her mind and said she loved him after all. He welcomed her back with great cries of hosanna. Then she changed her mind yet again, saying that in a relationship she could not *be*. Unable to comprehend the zigzag plot of this story, Michael lived at the end of her emotional yo-yo for six months until the string broke and she left for good. He grieved, and when his heart at last had mended, he found himself not embittered but with a larger and softer heart.

His second great love happened two years later with Marilyn, a divorced dance teacher at a neighboring school. They had met at a teachers' conference in the spring, and that summer, Michael would wait on his front porch for her to drive up to his house in Berkeley, her wild blond mane visible above the hedge as she emerged from her car. She pierced his heart with her goddess-like mastery of Tantric sexual practices and with the boundless generosity of her body and spirit. She was the most giving person he had ever known, a kind of sexual Mother Teresa. On his birthday of their first year together, she took him to a seaside cottage in Mendocino and initiated him into a Tantric ritual she had created especially for the occasion. It began with her blindfolding him to the sound of New Age music, proceeded through a ritual of furs and fabrics caressing his skin and enticing aromatic oils held under his nose, and ended two hours later with his near loss of consciousness in the most explosive orgasm of his life. What pierced his heart was not the cyclonic sex; rather, it was her generosity in creating for him such an elaborate gift.

During the two years that their relationship thrived, he believed he was at last living the happily-ever-after of his life story. But it fell apart when she began having recovered memories—drawn from the depths of her mind by a therapist—of being sexually abused as a young girl by her father. Though Michael assured her that he was willing to wait on her recovery for as long as it took and to do whatever he could to help, her soul had been seized by demons and she slammed the door on him forever. He grieved for a year and then began to heal. Again his heart became larger and softer, but he was also infected with a deep fear that the next woman he loved would turn out to be a shape-shifter like Marilyn.

What does it mean to say he had a larger and softer heart? A larger heart means one overflowing with love, like a cow's udder at milking time. A larger heart wants to give. A softer heart means one receptive and open, like a big catcher's mitt. Softer also means that Cupid's arrows could pierce his heart more easily. Some hearts are armored, so that even the most precisely shot arrow glances off. Michael's heart, for its size and softness, was a target as easy as a giant marshmallow.

Cupid's arrows are not universal; they are particular. It would be true—as a metaphor, of course—to say that an arrow has a certain person's name on it. Though Leanna's kiss would have aroused many men, it would have pierced the heart of only a few. Inflaming the genitals is different than piercing the heart. Exclaiming that she was so happy she could cry would have sent some men running for the exit, terrified of being responsible for another person's happiness. But Michael was waiting for just such a responsibility. Five years had passed since Marilyn had left him, and his cow's udder was near to bursting with love. His catcher's mitt was ready to receive such a pitch. His name, address, and phone number were written on her arrows. Her arrows were for him.

Leanna was his third and final love, the one that made sense of the other two. All the events of his life, from his first kindergarten crush to Marilyn's Tantric magic, through the circuitous route of two heartbreaks and the years of loneliness, were now redeemed and given meaning. Their meaning was that they led to Leanna. Along with meaning, metaphors, symbols, and poetic devices, stories have natural endings toward which everything flows and by which everything is defined. The meaning of Michael's story—the meaning of his life–was that it led to Leanna.

7

A few weeks before the start of the new school year, Michael drove over to the school to put his classroom in order. The quiet emptiness of campus in the summer made it seem like a dream world, peaceful and uncanny. As he was walking to his room, Jennifer called to him from across the lawn. When she caught up to him, they hugged. Jennifer taught Spanish and she was married to Kent, U.S. history teacher and basketball and baseball coach. They had joined the faculty the same year as Michael; from the beginning he had liked them both.

"If you have a few minutes, let's take a walk," Jennifer said, putting her hands around his forearm. Then she leaned close and lowered her voice. "I've got a couple of Axelrod stories for you, and I don't want the walls to hear."

Kay Axelrod was the school head, now in her eighth year and increasingly disliked by some of the faculty.

They walked along a trail that started at the edge of campus and wound through the redwoods of adjoining parkland. Dappled sunlight fell on the ferns growing between the trees.

"So what about Kay?" he asked. "I've gone the whole summer without school news. I need a gossip fix."

"There are two stories. The first is sort of funny. Well, sad-funny. You know the trip to India at the beginning of the summer, Kay and three faculty?"

"Sure, the grant and all that. Molly went."

It was an exploratory trip to plan an exchange program with a sister school in Mumbai. The trip was funded by a very wealthy trustee whom a few of the teachers privately called Daddy Warbucks. He was a venture capitalist with an array of business interests in India, and he had offered to fund a student exchange program.

"Molly's the one I heard this from," Jennifer said. "Molly had thought she was going to get to know Kay better on the trip. Bond."

"I remembering her saying that," Michael said, "though I can't understand why anyone would want to bond with Kay."

"You know Molly. Optimistic and upbeat. Well, they meet at the airport, and Molly asks about seats. She figures they can switch around a couple of times. Everybody eventually sits next to everybody. Like at a dinner party. Good manners. Democratic. With the layover in Japan, the whole flight was going to take over twenty-four hours. Well, it turns out the three teachers are sitting together in coach, and Kay has used her miles to upgrade to first class. They don't see her until they land, Kay looking fresh and relaxed from a good night's rest in her sleeper seat and her gourmet breakfast. And it's the same on the way back a week later."

"Unbelievable," Michael snorted. "But that's our Kay."

"That *is* Kay, isn't it? I don't think I had realized. Plus, I'm sure she accrued those miles traveling on school funds—all those conferences and things."

They paused to watch a squirrel run onto the trail, freeze at the sight of them, and then turn and scamper back. Jennifer giggled.

"But the other story is worse. You remember the big announcement last March—Kay is staying."

"Oh, yeah. The no-news news conference."

The previous spring, Kay had announced that she was a finalist for the headship at a prestigious school in Manhattan. Four days later the faculty was summoned to a meeting at morning break where a beaming chair of the board of trustees announced with great fanfare that Kay had agreed to stay. Though everyone applauded on cue, some of the faculty were disappointed that she was not leaving.

"So this summer," Jennifer began, "one of our colleagues—I can't tell you who, I was sworn to secrecy—meets someone from the Manhattan school at a conference and says, just to be jovial, oh, you almost stole our head away, blah, blah, blah. Well, bottom line, Kay was *not* a finalist. In fact, she spent a day there interviewing as one of five candidates and no one liked her. By lunch she had been crossed off their list."

Michael stopped on the trail, bent his knees and dropped his jaw. "She lied?"

"Well, yeah. Lied to our board, it would seem. But wait. Here's the clincher. Kay got a big salary increase for staying. She's going to be making 400 thousand this year."

"No! That's impossible."

"It's true," Jennifer said.

"Jesus Christ!"

"There's more."

"I can't take any more."

"The school bought her a car. Or bought a school car for her to use. A new BMW."

Michael put his palm to the side of his head. "She lives rent-free in a nice house, is furnished a car, and makes 400K... shit."

"I know. And teachers bake brownies for the auction to raise a few more dollars for the scholarship fund."

"How many people know about this?" Michael asked.

"Me and you. And Kent, of course. And my informant."

"You going to tell others?"

"I don't know. Kent thinks I should pretend I never heard it."

They walked awhile and paused to watch another squirrel, this one chattering at them from a branch of a redwood tree.

"I'm trying to remember," Michael said. "At the meeting. What exactly was the language? I mean, did they say she was a finalist? Or that she had an offer? Do you remember?"

"That's what I love about you English teachers," Jennifer laughed. "You always make us all get it right with the language." She thought for a minute. "I do remember that at the big announcement the board chair said that Kay had decided to stay. I remember that phrase: *decided to stay.*"

"You're right. I remember that, too. That's like me saying I've decided not to play shortstop for the Giants this season. Pretty much implies I could have. Plus, why would the board boost her salary so much if they didn't believe she was still in the running?"

Jennifer gave an exaggerated shrug.

At a fork in the trail they took the branch that looped back to campus. Strolling along the path, they talked about whether anything could be done. Jennifer thought someone on the board should be told. Both of them had taught students whose mothers or fathers were on the board. They wondered which ones might be sympathetic to faculty outrage.

Michael said, "The business about the plane ride to India—well, that's just Kay being Kay. But this other thing is a different matter. It's dishonest. It's fraud, really."

"You're right," Jennifer said.

They walked back to campus in silence.

When he told Jennifer about meeting Leanna, she turned to him and said, "I'm so happy for you." She was the kind of friend—the kind of person—who could utter the most clichéd saying with such sincere feeling that it sounded sacred. "I knew this would happen for you soon."

He told her about the age difference—blurted it, he felt—and waited for a response.

"It could be a challenge. But every relationship has challenges. If you love each other, you'll meet this challenge—and all the others. The people I worry about are those who don't know relationships always have challenges."

"Well, I certainly know it. I have my advanced degree from the college of hard knocks."

Jennifer looked at him and smiled. She and Kent had known Michael and Marilyn as a couple.

On the drive home Michael thought about Kay Axelrod. He loved the school; for twelve years now it had been central to his life. Since his mother had died, it had been even more an anchor, a kind of home. This news felt like a blob of black ink falling into a pool of clear water. It was what the Greeks called *miasma*: moral pollution. It did seem that someone should inform the board.

Michael had been hired at the school by John Johnson (whom students affectionately dubbed John-John), an East Coast boarding school veteran who came to California and started a new school. He had engineered the purchase of the campus of a military school whose mission made it a dying dinosaur in the post-sixties era. John was hard-working, generous, affable, and wise. He had a keen eye for good teachers, and he believed the formula for a successful school was great teachers and willing students. His philosophy of administration was "teachers know best." At its worst, that philosophy resulted in tedious faculty meeting debates about whether food should be allowed in the classroom or whether to dismiss before Christmas on Thursday or Friday; at its best, it made teachers feel valued and it built strong bonds of faculty loyalty to the school. John was loved.

Michael remembered one Saturday afternoon in October—he was in his third year of teaching there—when he settled in to grade student essays on his deck only to discover he had left them in his classroom. He drove over to the school as dusk was falling and there was a chill in the air. Walking to his office, he noticed a yellow glow coming from John's office. He walked past and saw John at his desk, writing with his favorite fountain pen, a half-eaten bag of store-bought cookies on his desk. Michel tapped lightly on the window and John waved him in.

John's office smelled wonderfully of fresh-brewed coffee, and he poured Michael a cup. He was writing college letters of recommendation for his secretary to type on Monday. He wrote one for every senior. He poured Michael a cup of coffee and pushed the cookie bag toward him.

"My wife thinks I should watch my diet, but I have to drink coffee to write these letters, and I can't drink coffee without eating cookies."

"Great coffee," Michael said, raising his mug in salute.

"Half a dozen cookies and I still can't get this letter quite right. I want to do a good one for her."

"Who is it?"

"Amanda."

"Still water runs deep," Michael offered.

"Ha!" John said, pointing at the pad. "That's exactly what I wrote. But I need an example."

"I might have one," Michael said. "This just happened a couple of weeks ago. There's this poem I teach in the European literature class. It's Rilke, 'Torso of the Archaic Apollo.' Like a lot of Rilke's poetry, it's intellectually challenging, but beyond that, it's deep in a spiritual way, and most students don't quite get it, or they just have a dim notion. I'm still working to completely get it myself."

Michael sipped his coffee. "The idea is that this piece of sculpture, or by implication any work of great art, has a level of being beyond what humans can achieve. So art can be thought of as judging us. Do we measure up? Well, Amanda got it. Really got it. And explained it enthusiastically. She was blushing the whole time, of course, but she explained it really clearly. She said this one thing. I remember it exactly. She said, 'Art is not just a beauty of appearance but a beauty of being.' That's the wisest, most succinct sentence I've ever read about that poem."

"Great stuff," John said, writing furiously, pausing only to push the cookie bag further toward Michael. Michael chuckled and took one. Apple spice. They were surprisingly good.

"That's why you're a great teacher," said John. "You draw that stuff out of kids."

"I don't know. I don't think I can take any credit for this one."

Now Michael replayed that scene in his mind. It was nine years ago, but as vivid as yesterday. Just a few months later—at February break—John had dropped dead of a heart attack. The next month, Kay Alexrod, who had connections to one of the board members, emerged as the new head. She had been working in the development office of another school. In the widespread grief and shock of John's death, the faculty had failed to claim a voice in the process of choosing the new head.

8

At times Leanna seemed so exuberantly happy to be with him that she bounced from room to room like a rubber ball. She had taken classes at a campus martial arts club, and at moments in the house, she would pause, pull her fists in to her chest, tilt her body sideways, and deliver a high kick into the air with one leg. She was a masterful cook with a gift for inventing delicious meals from whatever ingredients were around. Food was her natural medium for giving. She had a playful creativity about her, and when Michael showed her a pink stuffed elephant he had as a child, she named it "Fungus." It became a household pet to which each of them contributed pieces of a made-up personality and bits of Fungus lore. If Michael made a bad joke, Leanna turned Fungus around, lifted his tail, and made the sound of a Bronx cheer. Michael could never keep himself from laughing.

Leanna became curious about his camera, and he taught her how to use it. She became a photographer overnight, taking shots mostly of inanimate objects, showing a keen eye for pattern, geometry and the juxtaposition of objects in the everyday world: a row of roast ducks in the window of a Chinatown shop, an old man's hands holding chopsticks over a bowl, rows of peppers in a farmers' market. He gave her one of his cameras on permanent loan.

Though she seemed sexually inexperienced, their love-making was good, and he was able to give her orgasms. One night after they had made love, she whispered, "Tell me you love me." He did, his heart melting.

It seemed natural that their love must reshape their very names. Spontaneously, she began calling him Mikey. He named her Li-Li.

The new and wonderful twist that Leanna provided in the story of Michael's life did not prevent fears from darting through his mind like rats. His last two relationships had been invaded by demons he did not foresee. What if it happened again? What if Leanna became a shape-shifter? Before he experienced those two heartbreaks, he had thought that once love grew, it could not die without cause. If a man did not neglect or abuse his lover—in short, if he did not deserve to lose her—she would never leave him. He had believed in an orderly universe of justice governing love. Twice he had been proven wrong. Apparently the world of love was no more just or orderly than the cruel and chaotic world at large.

As he and Leanna fell more deeply in love, he felt reassured. When they had been together two months, she told him she had never loved anyone as deeply. He told her that he felt the same. He swelled with a warm sense of security. What does security mean? It means you are the author of your own story.

When he told her he had never loved anyone so deeply, was he telling the truth? Could he really love this woman he had known barely two months more than he had loved Marilyn after two years? It was true, but as an article of faith. It was belief *in* rather than belief *that*. It was the story he wanted to create.

There was a comfortable ease to their daily rhythm around the house, so when her apartment mates decided to give up their lease, it seemed natural for her to move in with Michael, just two months after the soul-shattering kiss. One afternoon they carried her belongings into his house—two suitcases, clothes on hangers, some cardboard boxes, and a tank with her pet snake named Clyde. They shopped for a desk and chest for her and assembled them together. She mailed in change-of -address forms. They cooked their first meal together. Frank came over for a drink and pronounced his blessing.

Although he felt reassured of her love, those rats of worry were forever waiting for an excuse to scurry through his mind. Her breakdown on the running trail proved to be prophetic. She stopped running because it reminded her of that day. If he asked how things were going at the lab and she didn't want to talk about it, she snapped at him. She was frequently tired, and when they made plans to go out, she might change her mind at the last minute. One morning after they got up, she looked in the mirror and said she felt like a "fat heifer," falling into a mood so dark he could not bring her out of it. She sulked around the house, and though she needed to return to the lab, she shut herself in the bedroom and did crossword puzzles. When he tried to cheer her up, she withdrew further. When he asked if she had ever been in therapy (almost everyone he knew had been in therapy), she felt insulted by the question and flew into a rage. During one of her dark moods, she told him that she was a bad person. She said it as if confessing to some corner of darkness in her soul.

During the one of their fights, he asked if she were trying to sabotage their relationship, and he wondered aloud if they were a match. She heard his remark as the beginning of a break-up speech, and she fell to the floor crying so hysterically that he was frightened. He cradled her in his arms and promised her that he would never leave her. This was the second arrow to pierce her heart–his promise of abiding and unconditional love.

Her moods also colored her sexuality. On some days she seemed aroused by him, but on other days she seemed not only sexually withdrawn but also averse to simple physical affection, complaining that his hugs made her too hot (it was a foggy sixty-two degrees!), or that he needed a shave, or that he had leaned against her arm and hurt it. She seemed not only sexually inexperienced, but also inept. In foreplay, instead of caressing his penis she grabbed and yanked it like the pull-rope in a belfry, causing him to wince in pain. Marilyn's body had seemed to say, let us dissolve the boundaries of our selves and merge in a bath of pleasure and love. Leanna's body seemed to say, I am separate from you; please observe visiting hours, subject to cancellation without notice, and don't climb on the furniture. Marilyn's volcanic orgasms had seemed to emanate from the depths of her soul; Leanna's seemed localized and quick, a kind of vaginal sneeze. Marilyn had lived fully *in* her body; Leanna seemed to live *behind* hers. To many men—and perhaps to Leanna's graduate school boyfriend—her sexual moodiness would have been a sharp disappointment if not a deal-breaker.

Why was this, or her overall moodiness, not a deal-breaker for Michael?

We do not wonder about Odysseus why the Cyclops, the wrath of Poseidon, or the terrible man-eating Scylla did not convince him to give up his quest for home. After all, he could have stayed with the beautiful Calypso in her idyllic cave and never grown old. We do not wonder because we accept the meaning of the story. It is Odysseus' destiny to return home. Could he have chosen otherwise? Yes, but at the price of no longer being Odysseus and his story no longer being *The Odyssey*.

So it was with Michael. Because the story he was now living had a plot (his whole life had led up to this), a quest (it was his mission to make Leanna so happy she could cry), a meaning (she was the defining love of his life), and an end (they would be together forever), any problems had the status of obstacles to be surmounted. Leanna was his Ithaka. Kurt Vonnegut said we only get to fall in love three times. This was Michael's third. This was it. As he said to Frank, "It's like a switch has been flipped. I'm committed. Forever." It was another way of saying that two arrows had pierced his heart, and the golden cords held him to her.

9

Michael looked forward to the start of the school year. Though the school year began in the last days of summer, the feeling was spring-like: fresh, full of renewal, stirring with new life. He loved receiving his schedule, the list of students enrolled in his classes, and the announcement about new faculty members. He loved writing the course syllabus and planning the first days of class. He liked shopping for just the right kind of notebooks. He liked to sharpen pencils just so he could smell them. There were always several days of faculty meetings—stale and boring—but the high point of those days for Michael was brief encounters with students who were on campus to buy their books, fill their lockers, change their schedules. Some of the underclassmen looked like they had grown six inches over the summer. Some of the boys had deeper voices. Jennifer told Michael there was a new spring in his step; the cause, of course, was his new life with Li-Li.

On the first morning of faculty meetings, Kay gave her annual "vision" address, intended to set forth some theme for the year. Usually, by the next day no one remembered what the theme was. But this year, her speech was more pointed. She had talked to an alum the previous spring who had gone to medical school, become a doctor, and then did not like it. "I'm afraid we are turning out students who are only good at school, and old school at that," she said. "We need to make classes more tailored to the real world." She concluded her speech with a pause for dramatic effect and then said, "We need to educate our students for their future, not our past." Michael thought he remembered reading the statement somewhere. Was she was quoting it without attribution?

Leaving the meeting, Michael fell into step with Keith Bluebeard, a young math teacher three years at the school. Keith was a good teacher, dedicated to his students but deliciously irreverent toward the school administration.

They exchanged eye-rolling looks.

"There's something about Kay…" Michael said with a shake of his head.

"I know what you mean," Keith answered.

"You do? What is it, then? Because I can't quite put my finger on it."

"She doesn't connect," Keith said. "It's like she's a robot giving a speech to other robots. Totally mechanical. So you start to feel like you're becoming a robot."

"Jesus. You hit the nail on the head. How do you do that? You're a math teacher. You're not supposed to know anything about people."

"She's not really a person," Keith laughed. "She's a bot."

"Ah. That explains it."

The afternoon speaker was Tim Morris, an education professor who had recently published a book, a manifesto for twenty-first century education. He began with the challenging assertion that today's schools, even the best, were not adequately preparing their students for the twenty-first century. He had interviewed a variety of high-tech CEOs who wanted in employees qualities not being taught in the schools.

His buzzwords were collaborative learning, thinking outside the box, being intentional, being interdisciplinary, and project-based learning. He said schools should create classrooms resembling the new workplace of the twenty-first century, not the classroom of the twentieth. Teachers should not teach but manage learning. In the classroom of the future, students would be learning on their computers while teachers walked around the classroom giving occasional aid. Michael got the feeling that in Mr. Morris' ideal school, everything that Michael valued about teaching the humanities would disappear.

Michael was sitting next to Jennifer, and she nudged his arm and tilted the screen of her open laptop in his direction. It was the speaker's web page, and Jennifer pointed to a line of text that explained he was the head of a special project at his university that was founded by the Gates Foundation.

His concluding words were, "We have to start making learning cool and contemporary. We have to start educating students for their future, not our past."

Jennifer elbowed Michael.

There was a reception for the speaker on the patio of the library, and Michael walked over with Jennifer.

"Kent had the right idea," Jennifer said. "He started baseball practice today."

"Ask him if he needs an assistant coach," Michael said. "Jesus. Usually Kay just bores me, but this time—with help from this Morris guy—she was downright insulting. And frightening. Or am I being oversensitive? Am I one of the 'resistant to change' people he talked about?"

"No," Jennifer laughed. "It *was* insulting. And disturbing. None of what she talks about is why I became a teacher."

At the reception, Kay was in her most charming mode, and she made a few remarks praising the speaker. When she said he had obviously inspired everyone, a few teachers exchanged glances. With warm enthusiasm she announced that the school had purchased a copy of his book for each teacher, and a copy would be placed in everyone's mailbox by the next morning.

10

Leanna's birthday was approaching. She had mentioned to Michael that her past few birthdays had been disappointing. No one had given her a cake (this seemed important to her), and the day had passed without due celebration. This news mobilized Michael as if he were a waiting army; he believed he could make her birthday so happy that she could cry.

She loved crossword puzzles, and the first film they had seen together was a documentary on the world of crosswords, so he set about making her a birthday crossword puzzle, using as the words names of restaurants they had visited, their private jokes and shared secrets, funny facts about Fungus, things only she would know. It went slowly, but he worked on it diligently in the hours they were apart. He ordered her a cake in her favorite flavor (mango mousse) with "Happy Birthday, Li-Li" written on it. He found a dress that looked like it was made for her—deep purple, light as gossamer, flowy, and feminine—and though it was expensive, he splurged. She had mentioned that it was her lifelong dream to go skydiving, so her found a skydiving site out in the valley and made a reservation for the morning of her birthday. For that evening he made a reservation at Berkeley's iconic Chez Panisse restaurant, thinking that if he decided to propose, it would be that evening at dinner.

Propose?

Yes. Though the soul-shaking kiss had been only two months earlier, did not his promise always to care for her imply—indeed, necessitate—marriage? And she had already hinted that she wanted to marry him, one day commenting that she had looked at the ring finger of her left hand and felt it naked.

Did he have doubts?

Yes, many.

She seemed to have a mean streak, and it was not unusual for her to make vitriolic remarks about people—usually women—because they were fat, or had bad hair, or were wearing something she found hideous. He couldn't understand it. She was blessed with a pretty face and a sexy, svelte body; why should the appearance of other women matter to her? One day in September, she drove over to Marin County to visit his school, and she sat in on one of his classes. She left seething with rage about the students, saying she wanted to burn their houses down and that it wasn't fair that they had led privileged lives while she had "suffered." It was true that most of his students were affluent (though some were on scholarship), but how had Leanna suffered? Her upbringing had been reasonably comfortable; indeed, in terms of material comforts, her background was little different than his own. Contrary to the stereotype some had about private schools, his students did not exude a sense of privilege; they were so appreciative that it was their habit, when they left the room after every class, to thank the teacher. Besides, affluence does not protect adolescents from an array of sufferings: parents with cancer, divorces, depression or anxiety, problems of self-esteem, even thoughts of suicide. When he tried to talk to her about this, she mentioned a girl who had been wearing expensive shoes, and then she became angry with him for not understanding her. The girl's expensive shoes were to Li-Li a symbol of her membership in a club, the club of people who possessed a sense of belonging. She felt Michael could not understand that.

Sex between them was becoming less frequent, and he wondered if she still found him attractive. It seemed that as soon as she had moved in, her libido had plunged, and her desire to make love with him now came once every week or two.

One evening after dinner—they were drinking tea, watching the sun set from the deck—she asked him for five words to describe her. He said, "Pretty, sexy, smart, charming, and egg-like: hard on the outside and soft in the center." He believed her to have something golden deep inside, a soft center of loving goodness, a core he had touched and been touched by. He did not tell her that at times she behaved like a tortoise, a jackrabbit, a porcupine, or a tiger. That is, she could close her hard shell and not let him in, she could bolt at great speed, she could put up sharp quills to keep him away, or she could lash out with sharp claws. But he believed in her golden center; it was an important metaphor in his story.

What was the evidence for her golden center? There wasn't much. But what is our evidence for the existence of God? It is scant. But we feel He *must* be there, so we believe. At least some do. Faith in Leanna's golden center was essential to Michael's story. He was a Believer.

Of course, he could have constructed a different story—a tragedy, for example, of one whose heart had been pierced by a woman who was impossible (too young, too immature, too bitchy). So why did he construct not a tragedy, but a romance like Odysseus finding home?

It may have been because of his mother, a woman who gave him love, attention, care (and discipline), and thus taught him by the time he was five that women were to be valued and trusted as sources of love. Why didn't his heartbreaking experiences with Elizabeth or Marilyn convince him otherwise? Because the first lesson is more deeply learned and thus not easy to erase. The first lesson sets the rule; subsequent conflicting lessons are exceptions.

So his decision to propose was not made by a weighing of pros and cons on a balance scale (the cons may well have weighed more). Remember that we said if Odysseus decided not to return home, he would not be Odysseus. Michael's decision was made to preserve his story, a story in which marriage to Leanna would be his homecoming. In his story, her happiness was his mission. When logic debates story, story is bound to win.

11

Meanwhile, what story was Leannna writing? Whatever it was, it was about to change. She had reached the end of her rope in the PhD program. The previous spring, an advanced math course—a course she hated—had given her great difficulty, and her advisor suggested she take it over. Though she had always done well as an undergrad, something about that course frightened her; parts of it seemed just beyond the limits of her mind and made her feel stupid. At her college in Texas, her happiest hours had been spent in the chemistry lab where her experiments succeeded, the work was fun and made her feel smart, and her professors praised her warmly. It was the source of her identity; she was known on the small campus as Leanna, superstar chemistry student. But now the experiments seemed boring, frustrating, and often unsuccessful. People worked on their own, and when she needed help, she could not bring herself to ask for it. She finally admitted it: she wanted to quit. Her jackrabbit impulse was to run.

If quitting her run up the fire trail had tormented her, this was a hundred times worse. As soon as she submitted her letter withdrawing from the program, she broke down. She sat on the floor of the bedroom and sobbed. Michael sat beside her and wrapped his arms around her. She did not melt into them;

instead, she remained tortoise-like, in her shell. "I'm a loser," she wailed. "I'm too stupid."

Michael sat with her and finally he told her something he remembered from the writings of Nietzsche, the metamorphoses of the human spirit through the stages of camel, lion, and child. The camel is the beast of burden, carrying the heavy load he's been given but never freely chose. "The PhD program had become that for you," he told her. The camel's refrain is *I must*. When the human spirit finds courage, it changes into a lion, a creature of courage with the strength to say *no*. "That's what you're doing," he said. "You have quit not because you're a loser, but because you found courage, because you became a lion." Finally, the lion finds something to say yes to and transforms into a child, saying *I am*. "That's yet to come," Michael said. When he got on all fours and roared, she giggled through her tears.

When her mother emailed the next week to say she hoped Leanna would change her mind and "realize her dreams," Michael pointed out that a PhD was her mother's dream for Leanna (worth a good rung or two on the ladder of life), not Leanna's dream for herself. Her mother wanted her to be a camel.

How was all this to be incorporated into Leanna's story of her life? Leanna was not an author of stories, properly speaking. Stories have a unity and a sense of meaning (as well as metaphors and poetic devices). Leanna was more a chronicler, like a ship's captain who daily keeps a log, recording the weather, the course of the ship, other ships sighted in passing. Of course, a ship's captain may well have a philosophic bent and start to reflect upon not just his destination, but also upon its meaning and purpose, but then his ship's chronicle would become a story. Because Leanna did not like to reflect on the meaning of life, she kept the diary of the chronicler. (Challenging her to be introspective could turn her into a tortoise, jackrabbit, porcupine, or tiger). In her chronicle of daily events, Leanna noted what happened and how she felt (happy, angry, frustrated, worried). For now her question was her destination in life, and she did not know the answer. She just knew that she had been defeated by the PhD program and felt like a quitter and a loser.

12

When Li-Li awoke on the morning of her twenty-sixth birthday, there was a card on the kitchen table. She had wondered about a present—from Michael there had been an aura of mystery—and she also wondered whether there would be a cake. In the card Michael expressed his undying love and his abiding commitment to her, and he announced that this would be a birthday of five presents, to be revealed throughout the day. The first was a Gerbera daisy, her favorite flower, and it was in a vase before her on the breakfast table. After reading the card, she threw her arms around him and cried softly from happiness. That first arrow that had pierced his heart on the night of the pomegranate cocktail was now planted in his heart like a tree, its roots growing every time he made her so happy she could cry.

Then he gave her the crossword, and she set about working on it with delighted laughter. After breakfast, he handed her the wrapped box. She tore off the paper and held up the dress. She stood, stripped off her sweatpants and top, and slipped the dress over her head. She ran to the mirror, stood on her tiptoes, spun, twirled, posed, pranced and sashayed, basking in the prettiness of her image.

Michael told her told her to dress for an athletic event, and they drove an hour out to the skydiving center. Just as she was beginning to complain about the length of the drive, they pulled into the parking lot and she saw the sign, her eyes again filling with tears.

They were handed several pages of release documents. When Michael got to the part stating, "parachutes and other equipment may not function as intended," he stopped reading and signed. They were fitted for their flight suits and harnesses, given instructions, and with ten other people they boarded an old twin-engine propeller plane that looked like something from an aviation museum. On board, they were given a review of their instructions, and then everyone sang Leanna happy birthday—loud and deliberately off-key.

When the plane reached twelve thousand feet, it leveled off. Michael had purchased a video of their jump, and it would reveal Leanna beaming with the excitement of a child, Michael with the corners of his mouth pulled down in dread. If this was as safe as they had told him on the phone, why did he have to sign release forms longer than his home mortgage documents? In his enthusiasm for Leanna's birthday, he had not stopped to think exactly what skydiving would be like. Now the reality that he was about to jump out of a plane hit him like a kick in the stomach. He tried to steady himself by looking at Li-Li's face, drawing courage from the happiness he read there.

Michael was strapped in front of his tandem instructor by a harness, checked and double checked, and reminded of his instructions. When the pilot yelled back into the plane that they were nearing the jump zone, Michael's heart leapt against the side of his chest like a caged rabbit trying to escape. Then he and his instructor duck-walked in tandem toward the plane door. Leanna and her instructor were right behind him. Michael turned and tried to smile, but she was adjusting her goggles and laughing, and he failed to catch her eye. He had wondered if it would be hard to make himself jump, but as he watched the videographer climb onto the wing, he realized that since he was in front of his instructor, she would do the jumping and he would essentially be pushed from the plane.

They stood in the door. He looked down, the instructor gently pulled his head back, and they jumped. The feeling was unlike any he had ever experienced—a plunging sensation, streaking speed, and the loud rushing noise of the wind. At the instructor's signal, he extended his arms as he dropped belly down through the cold air at 120 miles per hour, trying to get his breath. He could feel his checks flapping like flags in a hurricane. After about sixty seconds of free fall, the instructor shouted into his ear that she was about to deploy the chute, and he was jerked upward into stillness. Now he felt he was barely moving at all. They floated quietly, the air growing warmer as they descended. When he watched the videotape the next day, he would see that at this moment he turned his head and said something to his instructor, but he was unable to remember what he had said. It seemed important, and though he tried, he could not recall it.

They landed gently and he fell softly on his side. Ten seconds later Leanna landed on the other side of the field, her instructor so adept that they stepped onto the ground as if getting off of a bus. Li-Li ran to Michael and they hugged, and the still photograph of that instant would hang above his desk at school in the coming year.

Back home, he made lunch and gave her the mango mousse cake. When she blew out the candles, he wondered if her wish had anything to do with him. Later that afternoon, Michael removed from the hiding place his grandmother's engagement ring. They were beautifully cut diamonds, and his grandmother had always told him that the ring was to go to his wife.

A sliver of indecision was still with him; perhaps he should wait six months, see how things went, weigh the pros and cons. The more cautious approach made a lot of sense. But what are caution and sense in the face of a story? He put the ring in his pocket, feeling like he was stepping out of another plane.

Li-Li wore her new purple dress, and when they entered the dining room at Chez Panisse, she whispered to him that he looked handsome. He told her looked beautiful. In this moment, his life story seemed to have become an enchanted fairy tale. For Li-Li, she no longer felt like a country mouse. She felt visible. She felt she belonged. She felt cared for. She felt happy.

They tasted their wine, a straw-colored chardonnay, and talked about the mysterious way—indecipherably so, to them—in which wines were described.

Michael took another sip and said, "I like it—a lot—but I don't believe I taste hints of pear or melon."

"Did the waiter really say 'crushed marble'?" Li-Li asked.

"Yes, he did. That's a new one on me."

"Be careful you don't chip a tooth," she said.

They agreed they needed a new system, and Michael suggested breeds of dog. Leanna liked the idea, and they each took a long, contemplative sip. They put down their glasses and looked at each other. Then at the same instant, they both said "collie" and burst out laughing.

If that's not a sign we should marry, Michael thought to himself, I don't know what would be. Ever after, when they said the same thing at the same time, they would look at one another and repeat the word *collie*.

After they had finished their main course of duck breast, Michael excused himself as if to go to the restroom, found their waiter, and gave him the ring. A few minutes later, the table across the room received dessert with a candle, and when the waiter put down Leanna's dessert plate, she said with the resentment of the ignored, "Why didn't *I* get a candle?" It was her birthday; why hadn't Michael informed the waiter?

Smiling, Michael shrugged and watched her. She continued frowning across the room at the other diner's candle, piqued at the unfairness of it. Then she looked down at her plate. She paused, as if paralyzed by a puzzle she could not solve. Seconds passed. Then recognition bloomed, and she covered her mouth with her hand.

"Will you marry me, Li-Li?" he asked.

"Yes," she said and began to cry.

The arrow in her heart—that here was a man who knew how to care for her—was quivering in happiness.

At home, he thought that the perfect end to their day would be to make love. It had been over a week. But she opened her computer so she could post pictures of her birthday and her engagement on her social media page, her ship's chronicle. Michael waited for her in bed, letting the great import of the day sink in. He again tried to remember what he had asked the instructor just after the chute had opened, but he couldn't recall it. Where do our lost memories go? he wondered. Do they evaporate like dew or seep into the ground like rain? He let the other memories of the day pass through his mind, the better to savor them. Li-Li's time on the internet stretched on and on, and finally he fell asleep.

PART TWO:
IN SICKNESS AND IN HEALTH

1

Michael always started his freshman English course with *The Catcher in the Rye*. Early on, students fell into two camps: a minority loved Holden and saw something of themselves in him, while the majority derided him as a loser who failed exams, lacked good friends, and only found fault. "He's a total misfit."

Michael let them have their say, and then he asked questions to subvert the majority view.

"So Holden doesn't like anything?" Michael asked, holding his white board marker.

"No, nothing. He hates everything and everybody."

"You're sure?" Michael asked.

Silence. The students shifted in their seats and thumbed the pages.

"Can anyone find anything in the text that he *does* like, even if it's unconventional?"

"The snow." It was a girl who hadn't spoken much. Michael asked her to read aloud the passage in which the newly fallen snow looks so pretty that Holden decides not to throw a snowball and mess it up. He wants to preserve the perfect beauty of the snow.

One by one, students found that there *are* people he likes— Phoebe, his dead brother Allie, and Jane, so quirky that when playing checkers she keeps her kings in the back row. And the nuns. And the modest and earnest kettle drummer at Radio City Music Hall who is innocent of the flashy showmanship of Ernie, the piano player in the Village. Little kids who are nice and polite. Michael wrote on the board the list of things Holden likes. A shift began to occur. Of course Holden was wrong to smoke cigarettes and skip his homework, but maybe his value as a character lies in what he reveals about our world. Did they know any boys like Stradlater? Glances were exchanged. Phonies? Some nodded. Didn't Stradlater just want to use Jane, whereas Holden cared for her? This got the girls' attention. Some of the boys looked sheepish. Weren't *use* and *care* opposing ways of relating to the world, whether the environment or other people? Michael gave them lots of time to talk about that.

On the last day of the unit, Michael distributed a photocopied opinion piece from *The New York Times* arguing that *Catcher* was dated. Several high school students and a couple of teachers were quoted as saying Holden's passivity had no relevance in a world where students are working hard to get into top colleges. A teacher said the text was dated. The punch line of the article was a quote from a student who wanted to "tell Holden to shut up and take his Prosac." Michael's students were incensed. Couldn't those students empathize with people who might be sad or depressed? Michael nodded. One student fumed, "How could a *teacher* miss the point of the book, for Chrissakes?" Michael broke into a broad grin. After class he walked across the campus with a bounce in his step.

One morning in late September, Michael was sitting at his desk looking over two poems he would teach in his next class when three freshmen girls frantically burst into his room to say that Anya thought she had OD'd on speed, and should they call 911?

After Michael placed the 911 call, his students led him to the far side of the gym where Anya was sitting on the ground sobbing, her fists clenched. She had snorted meth in the bathroom but had not dripped, and now her heart was racing and she was panicked. She looked even more terrified when she heard the approaching siren. Michael placed his hand on her shoulder and talked to her in a calm voice, assuring her that she would be okay. The paramedics set down their cases and took over.

They let him ride in the ambulance with her. Her pulse was racing, and the heart monitor read 140, but the paramedic was reassuring. Michael noted with relief that they drove to the hospital without the siren. After they wheeled Anya into the emergency room, she was given an IV. Once she was stable and had calmed down, Michael sat beside her bed and they talked. Schools are anthologies of stories, and she told him hers.

Anya was a quiet, shy girl, a scholarship student with uneven academic skills but a sharp intelligence. She had a look of soulful vulnerability that drew some of the other students to her in friendship. They reacted to her vulnerability not with sadistic aggression, but with warm acceptance and gentle care. It was that kind of school—exactly as John Johnson had wanted it to be. Anya's mother had emigrated from Nepal when Anya was six. The father was an American who had since moved by himself to New York.

In the past month Michael had noticed that Anya, usually shy and reticent in class, had become lively, energetic, and engaged, and she had come out of her shell more with other students. Now he knew why. Daily meth, in careful, moderate doses, had boosted her energy and her confidence.

When Anya's mother arrived at the hospital, worried, distressed, and embarrassed, Michael tried to console her with the Jewish proverb that sometimes a stumble prevents a fall. This was Anya's stumble. She would eventually be better for it. She was a good kid. The mother seemed heartened to hear this.

Michael took a cab back to school. He thought he should check in with Kay Axelrod to let her know how Anya was doing. She motioned him into her office, and before he could say anything, she stood up and exclaimed with alarm and outrage, "Do you know they've already heard about this over at Oak Hills?"

Oak Hills was one of their feeder schools, a K-8 private school with a particularly well-heeled parent body. It was where Kay had worked in the development office prior to being made head at Michael's school. Kay had already talked to the police, and the last thing she told Michael was, "For God's sake, don't tell anybody it was meth." The subtext was clear: drugs are bad enough, but we don't want anyone to associate our school with a ghetto drug. Michael teetered with existential vertigo, so close was he to saying, "Don't bother asking whether Anya's dead or alive, Kay. Because all you care about is the school's reputation and your own goddamned resume."

The incident reignited his outrage over Kay Axelrod's scam with her job offer last year. A moral pollution was present, but unlike in Thebes, there were no barren women or dying crops, just an intangible corrosion that Michael felt like a burn on his skin. So when Jennifer invited him to a meeting of a few teachers to discuss what to do about Kay, Michael did not hesitate. Jennifer, with input from Kent, who did not want to be included, had put together a "Gang of Five."

When Michael arrived at Kent and Jennifer's, he saw that the five included, in addition to Jennifer and himself, Jim, Peggy, and Keith Bluebeard. Jim, the biology teacher, was a twenty-year veteran who had two daughters in the school, one a junior and the other a freshman. A *nice guy* in the best sense of the term, he did not have an enemy in the school. Peggy was the seventy year-old Latin teacher, hired by John Johnson in the school's first year, earthy, impish, and endlessly energetic. She reminded Michael of his mother. Keith Bluebeard, the young math teacher was the fifth. All present had won the annual outstanding teacher award, Keith just the previous spring; Peggy had won it twice.

After the coffee had been poured and freshly baked chocolate chip cookies passed, Kent excused himself, saying that one person in the household needed to keep his job. Nervous laughter followed. The mood was a mixture of giddiness and unease, giddy that they were doing something forbidden and uneasy that this could involve some risk.

Jennifer had told each person the story of Kay's apparent deception about her not-so-near job offer. She asked everyone to state what, if anything, they thought should be done.

Peggy recalled the time during the school's seven-year accreditation when the visiting accreditation team held drop-in meetings with the faculty. To that committee Peggy had voiced her concerns about communication and transparency, how the faculty often felt in the dark about decisions made by the administration. When the session ended, one of the other faculty members present had apparently walked over to Kay's office and reported what had been said. There were a couple of real sycophants on the staff. The next morning Peggy was called into Kay's office. Trying her best to be civil, Kay said she just wanted to hear Peggy's concerns. With icy politeness, she said that she was disappointed that Peggy had expressed her concerns to the accreditation committee rather than to her.

"I have always felt intimidated by her," Peggy said, "especially since that meeting. She's always reminded me of the tall, blond, mean girls in my own high school."

"I wonder why," Keith said drolly. "Kay is only all three of those."

Peggy added, "I feel nervous just being at this meeting." Then she added with a tiny laugh and tears welling up in her eyes, "A part of me thinks she's got this room bugged and I'll get fired tomorrow."

As Peggy wiped her eyes, a pall settled over the meeting. Jennifer patted Peggy's hand.

"My problem with her isn't a single incident," Jennifer said. "It's everything. Like the way she treats her secretaries. What's it been—five in eight years? She berates them for things that aren't even their fault. This is a school. Everything in it should be a model of what kind of people we want students to be— even the stuff they never see."

Keith Bluebeard was succinct: "I think what I've always thought: She's the Wicked Witch of the East, out for herself first, and second, for the rich people she wants to be one of. But unless we can get eighty per cent of the faculty walking a picket line—and I don't think we could get two per cent— there's nothing we can do."

There was a shifting of weight in the chairs, and then Jim said, "I think we need to sit down with the Board, or a committee of it. I believe there's a subcommittee responsible for evaluating the head. I don't think it would serve the school to do anything radical and sudden, but whenever Kay's current contract is up, they could just not renew it. This is her eighth year—that's already more than the average head's tenure these days, isn't it? That way she can find a new job and we can have plenty of time to find a new head, and there will be a minimum of disruption all around."

Michael told of Kay's comment the day Anya was taken to the hospital. Then he said, "It seems like everything we've identified are not just mistakes, or a matter of some policies that need to change. It's really just who she is."

Jennifer said, "So everybody thinks that should be our goal—that she needs to go?'

There were slow nods all around.

"A leopard can't change its spots," Peggy said.

They decided to send two of their number to speak with Barbara Smith, the board president. She was a CEO, and they believed her to be a person of integrity. It was decided that Jennifer and Jim would approach her.

2

Michael thought about his coming responsibilities as a husband. For some men, such responsibilities would seem, if not an outright burden, at least a heavy load, a great weight to be borne on strong legs. Think ox, camel, burrow, or pack horse. Michael did not feel marriage responsibilities a burden at all; they seemed like the air through which he would soar like a bird in flight. In matters of love, it is commonly said that timing is everything. Michael was ready.

He wrote Ma a letter of self-introduction, promising that he would always love and care for Leanna. Ma did not like the letter; she told Leanna it was "too direct." Though his finances were sound, a life insurance policy would provide a safety net for Leanna should something happen to him, so he phoned the company that administered the school's retirement account and signed up for a policy large enough to require a physical.

A few days after the medical exam, he got a call from his doctor saying that, though it was probably nothing to worry about, his PSA level had tested a bit high and she was sending him to a urologist. Michael's grandfather had died of prostate cancer, so he was worried. He tried to replay the doctor's voice in his memory to discern how candid her "nothing to worry about" statement sounded.

A few days later he talked with a friend who a couple of years earlier had a similar scare, with a higher PSA than Michael's, and the verdict had been good—no cancer. "But the needle biopsy isn't fun," he warned. He was right. A locally applied anesthetic deadened most of the pain, but to Michael the experience was like having a staple gun stuck up his rectum and fired into his prostate gland fourteen times. He could feel the vibrations into his skull. Afterwards, he tried to put the ordeal and the coming lab report out of his mind.

One evening when he and Li-Li were halfway through dinner (he had grilled salmon), the phone rang. It was the urologist telling him that he had prostate cancer.

He returned to the table feeling like he had stuck his finger in an electrical outlet. He told Li-Li and watched the blood drain from her face. They pushed the rest of their food around their plates in silence.

Later that night he sat down with Li-Li to talk. He told her that she had not bargained for this, and that if she wanted out of their engagement and their relationship, he would let her go without thinking less of her. She was young and pretty, and her future with him was now uncertain: things could turn out well, or they could slide into a nightmare of chemotherapy, declining health, and worse. Prostate cancer kills 29,000 American men each year. He could be one of them.

He had taken a step back from her in order to say it, and Li-Li did not like the backward step. Her instinct was to clutch onto him with a fierce strength, to save him from cancer, from death. She did not hesitate. She would stay with him no matter what. A third arrow pierced his heart.

It is true: Whether a friend, colleague, lover, spouse, or family relative, the person who will stay with you when things turn bad—or threaten to turn bad—is a rare and precious find.

Michael knew how precious. He now believed in the depths of his heart that Li-Li was just such a jewel.

Prostate cancer, he would learn, is the second most common form of cancer in American men. Age is a major risk factor. Of men diagnosed with prostate cancer, 97% are fifty or older. At forty, Michael was a rare case. But genetics is another risk, and his grandfather's prostate cancer was likely a factor. When he and Li-Li met with the urologist a few days later, the doctor explained that Michael's young age and his family history could indicate that his cancer was the more dangerous and rapidly spreading variety, but there was no further test that could tell. Surgery was deemed to be the best strategy, and his chances of remaining cancer-free afterwards, while not guaranteed, were fairly good. The surgery was scheduled for the following month. At the end of the meeting, Leanna asked the doctor what she should cook for Michael for his recovery.

Because the surgery would render him infertile (the prostate gland supplies the fluid in which the sperm swim), Michael began to pay visits to the sperm bank. He and Li-Li agreed that they wanted to have children—he wanted one; she was thinking two. She had even chosen names: Chloe for a girl and Mason for a boy.

The sperm bank was housed in a nondescript concrete building that looked like a survivalist's bunker. Because the sign in front contained the organization's initials, not its name, Michael walked past the building twice before realizing what it was. After talking with the counselor and filling out pages of legal and medical forms, he was sent into a small room to make his first "deposit." It looked like a half-sized college dorm room furnished with what seemed like a thrift store chair, a single bed, and a small bookshelf stocked with soft-core porn magazines. He half expected a masseuse in red lingerie to open the door. Though Michael had been an enthusiastic masturbator since he was thirteen, and coming of age sexually in the post-sixties generation had purged him of any Puritanism, he felt defiled by the setting. He thought of Li-Li, and of their Eurasian baby—Chloe or Mason—and he wished there were something more soulful and sacred in the room, like candles and an alter. He felt a deep pang of regret that their baby-making had to begin like this, Li-Li not even present. He felt he was letting Leanna down as her husband. For the first time, felt diminished as a man by the cancer diagnosis.

After some difficultly in getting started, he resorted to one of the magazines and finished the job. He was disturbed to see blood still in his semen, an after-effect of the needle biopsy. He diligently went to the sperm bank twice a week for the next month, and Li-Li thanked him for his efforts. Neither felt like joking about it.

3

One of the school's policies of which Michael felt proud was the rule that any student voluntarily reporting a drug problem for himself or for another student would not be met with disciplinary measures but rather with counseling help. The policy had been instituted years ago by John Johnson. It had rescued more than one student from wading into a morass. When students had come to Michael the morning of Anya's crisis, they showed that the policy worked, for they did not have to weigh getting her help against getting her in trouble. The following week Anya's teachers received an email from Deb Schmidt, the dean of students, saying that Anya would not be returning.

Michael was suspicious. That afternoon the same three students who had asked Michael to call 911 that morning came into his room to tell him that Anya had met with Dean Schmidt and been "counseled out" of the school. Michael sent Deb an email, and that afternoon, not having received a reply, he walked over to her office, his stomach churning. He had tried to think about the best way to begin, but when the door closed he said simply, "Whose decision was it? "

She looked at him blankly and said, "It was an administrative team decision." By the way she swallowed the sentence at the very moment she spoke it, Michael knew she was lying. It had been Kay's call.

In a firm voice, Michael said, "The purpose of the policy was the welfare of the students. It tells them that if they are slipping into something dangerous, they can tell us and we will help them, not expel them. It worked. It might have saved Anya's life. This decision tells them they'd better not come to the adults on campus for help. Surely you know this. Doesn't Kay know it?"

Deb seemed unready for this question.

"Plus," Michael added. "We are going back on our own commitment. What kind of message does that send? Where's the morality in it?"

Deb's face reddened, and then her eyes moistened. Michael wasn't in the mood to let her off the hook.

"John Johnson started that policy," he said. "He would turn over in his grave if he knew of this."

"It's not John's school anymore, Michael."

"It never was John's school, and he never wanted it to be. That's one of the reasons he was a really good head. He was the school's steward, not its goddamned czar. And it's not Kay's school now, thank God. That's the whole point. The school is the school. It's larger than any single administrator. It's not somebody's sandbox—or resume."

Michael was still standing, and Deb sat behind her desk, her face gray now.

Michael continued. "Not only are we violating policy that in the long haul protects the safety of the students, but we're breaking a promise. Where's the school's integrity?"

"I just can't do anything for you on this one," Deb said, her mouth pinched. This seemed to be the only thing she could think to say.

"So should I take this up with Kay?" he asked.

"I wouldn't advise it, Michael. I really wouldn't."

Michael turned on his heels and walked out of her office. For the first time in his adult life, he felt he was a hair's breadth from picking up a chair and smashing it into the wall. When he unlocked his car door, he realized his hands were shaking.

I can't do anything for you on this one. Driving home, Michael thought about the various ways in which that was an idiotic sentence. He wondered whether he should have stayed in Deb's office longer and argued with her. Would she have just kept repeating the same thing? He also wondered what was behind her advice not to take it up with Kay. Would Kay go ballistic? Or was it just futile? When he told Li-Li what had happened, she joined him in his rant.

4

When Marilyn had become a shape-shifter and ended their relationship, Michael saw a therapist in search of relief from his heart-wrenching grief. The therapist was helpful, but very expensive, and in some of their sessions she seemed to do little more than listen, occasionally rephrasing and repeating something he had said. Eventually Michael invented a kind of self-therapy. In the rear corner of his backyard, behind the cottage, was a large, flat stump of a redwood tree that had been cut down before he bought the house. Beside it sat a galvanized metal garbage can with a secure lid containing his emergency earthquake kit: energy bars, a flashlight, a thermal blanket, a small radio and a package of batteries, first aid supplies, and a five gallon jug of distilled water. He had added a baseball that he had retrieved one day when it nearly hit him on the head as he walked past the stadium on the Berkeley campus. He thought of this baseball as a kind of lucky talisman. (It had fallen from the heavens and blessed him by missing his head.) Whenever he felt the need for a therapy session, he went to his backyard, sat on the stump, took out the baseball, and talked aloud to it for a focused half hour. The sessions actually helped, and they were free. He had never told anyone, not even Li-Li, about his secret ritual. Now, for the first time in several years, he sat on the redwood stump and revolved the baseball in his hands. When he spoke, he said in a cracking voice that took him by surprise, "Please don't let cancer take me away from Li-Li."

The gravity of his diagnosis was driven home when he received an email from one of his old wedding clients asking if he could shoot her sister's wedding the following summer. That very morning he had heard on the radio that a former baseball star, one he had idolized as a boy, had died of prostate cancer. Realizing the uncertainty of his health, he wrote back his apologies saying he was already booked for that date. He bought a do-it-yourself kit and made out a will. He told Li-Li where it was kept. She didn't want to hear it.

His story was clearly at a junction. But the metaphor of a junction suggests a choice. There is a fork in the road; shall I go left or right? Take the road less traveled or the road more traveled? Asking Li-Li to marry him had been a choice. His cancer was not a choice. Li-Li's deciding to stay with him after his cancer diagnosis had been her choice. Navigating this junction was more like clinging to a raft in a swollen river that splits into two. Whether you go to the right of the island or to the left is decided by where the current carries you. You can try to paddle, but you delude yourself if you think it affects the outcome. He had not created his cancer. Whether the cancer had spread would not be his choice. His story was out of his control.

But aren't stories made up? Isn't that why we call the genre fiction?

Not even fiction is entirely made up. Its ingredients are of life and this world. If humanity had evolved on Mars, red desert poems would be big, not pastoral poetry with green moss and babbling brooks. Or if there were such poetry, it would be called science fiction. And on earth, if humans had evolved in such a way that love and sex did not exist (if people reproduced asexually, like growing second teeth), then the history of literature would be significantly altered. *Romeo and Juliet* would just be an Elizabethan Hatfields and McCoys story.

In the opening lines of *The Odyssey*, Odysseus is described as *polytropos*, a word that can mean "much turned" or "much turning." Things happen to him, and he makes things happen to others. Every life has that dual nature. Michael's life—and story—was much turned by his cancer diagnosis as it had been by the demons that made Marilyn a shape-shifter. But there were things he could do; he was "much turning," choosing surgery by a specialist skilled in the latest techniques of robotic prostatectomy, banking his sperm for a future child. There was also the issue of Li-Li.

One afternoon he sat on the redwood stump contemplating the red thread in the seams of the baseball. He asked aloud whether his relationship with Leanna was a train he should step off of. Yes, Li-Li had said she was committed to stay with him, and he was grateful for it. But was he being selfish? His cancer was not the only problem. Thinking about his cancer heightened his sense that the sands were running out on him. He was forty now and she had just turned twenty-six. Though he was active, athletic and lean, a healthy eater, and forever young at heart (thanks to his students), he was older by a decade and a half. When she was forty-five, presumably a healthy middle-aged woman, he would be almost sixty. Suppose he died when Mason or Chloe was only sixteen—or six? Suppose his cancer had already metastasized?

Even if his cancer were cured, he would grow old first. Was this best for her? Was he being fair? If he were to act from selfless generosity and far-seeing wisdom, would he not end their relationship now, a kind of lover's sacrifice of Abraham? She would be terribly hurt, of course, but she would get over it in a few months. Would not a lifetime with a more age-suitable mate be worth a few months of heartache? Should he turn his life story into a tragedy of noble sacrifice: his happiness sacrificed for hers?

On the other hand, would it not be arrogant to believe he could judge what was best for her? He had told her she could leave, and she had chosen to stay. She was an adult. Did he not owe her the respect of accepting her decision? Nor can the future be predicted. He could recover from his cancer and in two years she could be stricken with leukemia; then he would be the one nursing her. In ancient Hebrew, the common metaphor for the past is looking in front of us; the future is behind us, where we can't see it. About the future, we can only attempt a reasonable calculation of the probabilities. But we don't live the probable; we live the actual. We have Oedipus to warn us against the belief that we can shape our own fate.

As he gripped the hard, round baseball in his hand, another thought occurred to him. He had been thinking of this as an issue of two entities: himself (was he being selfish?) and herself (what course of life was best for her?). But there was a third entity now, a new character to their story: *them*, the couple of Mikey and Li-Li, later to be joined by Chloe and Mason, a nascent family, a whole greater than the sum of the parts.

We cannot talk about wholes and parts without recalling that charming myth related by Aristophanes in Plato's *Symposium*. Humans were originally round, having four hands, four feet, and two faces, and "terrible was their strength and swiftness." Fearing this power, the gods split them into halves and tied up the split skin at the navel, leaving each creature to roam the earth looking for its other half. When a reunion occurs, we call it love. Were not he and Li-Li now a union he had no right to challenge?

Sitting on the redwood stump, Michael felt like a debating society was meeting inside his head.

In the end, his story was moving like a train on which he was part passenger, part engineer. We tell our stories, but at times, stories tell themselves, leaving us to listen. Watching the countryside slide past, he could worry and wonder, but he could not step off of his own story, nor could he lay new track. Her happiness was his mission, and his heart was bound to her by three cords attached to three arrows. That was all he knew.

5

One of the job applications Li-Li had submitted came through, and she started work as a junior chemist at a start-up company developing battery technology. A number of the people who worked there were in their twenties or thirties, some of them recent PhDs from Berkeley. The work culture was casual and friendly. The HR person brought her dog to work, and several times a day Li-Li visited the dog to give it tummy rubs. There were couches to lounge on, a movie-and-pizza night once a month, and occasional lunch-hour soccer games in the parking lot. Her pay and benefits were good, and the job made her feel adult, responsible, and useful. People are defined not only by their dreams, but also by their nightmares. One of Li-Li's nightmares was being useless. For now she felt useful. She felt affirmed and happy. She was on a higher rung of the ladder. There was a guaranteed daily entry into her ship's log.

One day on her lunch hour, she stopped by the chemistry department at Berkeley to say hello and tell people about her job. One of her ex-classmates had quit the program, and another was applying to law school. Two students a year ahead of her had just failed their prelims. A fifth-year student was rumored to have taken an overdose of sleeping pills. One of the recent PhDs had failed to find a job and was waiting tables in

San Francisco. Their stories made her feel less a quitter and a failure. Maybe Michael had been right. Maybe she was a lion.

Michael's cancer frightened her. She was not so much afraid that he might die (somehow she was sure that he would not), but she was afraid that he might change. Suppose he became depressed or less caring of her? The good care he took of her was the first arrow that had pierced her heart. The second was that he loved her unconditionally. He was like an anchor. What if the cancer caused those two things to change? Suppose the anchor pulled loose and left her adrift? To think about his cancer was to give in to it. She would not think about it.

6

When the Gang of Five met again, Jennifer and Jim reported on their meeting.

"Barbara met us on a Saturday morning for breakfast," Jim said, "She was certainly polite and cordial, and she seemed concerned, but she kept her cards very close to the vest. Neither of us could tell what she was thinking."

Jennifer added, "We focused on the bogus job offer, but we made it clear that there were other concerns. We told her that faculty morale was low. We told her it might be time for a new head, someone more like John Johnson. A week later, she asked us over to her house. Beautiful house, immaculate, right out of a magazine." She laughed, "I felt like I should have dressed better just to walk in the door. We thought something significant was up. But she told us it had probably been a misunderstanding, and basically to forget it."

Keith Bluebeard laughed out loud.

"Misunderstanding?" Peggy cried.

"Yes," said Jennifer. "I listened very carefully and those were the key words: *probably* and *misunderstanding*."

"What was the misunderstanding?" Michael asked. "Did we misunderstand Kay, or did Kay and the school in New York have a misunderstanding… or was it Kay and the board?"

"We don't even know," Jennifer said, looking into her lap.

"We should have challenged it more," Jim said. "But, I don't know. Sitting in the living room of her mansion, her husband being jovial and friendly, I found myself nodding and smiling a lot. Barbara seemed so uncomfortable that I found myself feeling sorry for her. After I left, I felt like I had just been sold something I didn't want. Riding home in the car, I thought of the arguments I should have used. I felt like I failed to do a very good job as an advocate for faculty interests. The more I have thought about it, the more I've felt like a rube."

"Me, too," Jennifer said. "I feel like I let you guys down."

The rest of the group was quick to reassure them.

"It's class solidarity," Keith Bluebeard said quietly. "I know I sound like a broken record, but I just believe they will stick with Kay no matter what. Why do you think there's no faculty member on our board? Lots of private schools have them. I doubt there's anyone on the board who makes less than 500K a year."

Keith's perspective had always seemed extreme, but now the extreme was making sense.

A few days later Michael and Jennifer had lunch together.

"I feel terrible about my role in the Gang of Five. Kent thinks I'm crazy to think that."

"I agree with Kent—you're crazy. It would have gone the same way with any of us there. I mean, the board had already decided. Any logical case we made was going to be irrelevant. What could you have done? Except throw a tantrum, and what good would that have done? I think Keith is right. This is just raw power. They have power and we don't."

"I don't want to believe that."

"When John Johnson was head it was different. It was like a family. Now it's like a corporation—cold and hard."

"Kay has certainly destroyed my beliefs about female leaders being more humane." Jennifer said.

They ate in silence for a while. Suddenly Jennifer suddenly said, "Wow. I just remembered something."

Michael looked up at her.

"Because of what you said about power. Years ago, during Christmas break, Kent and I were going to have a little dinner party, but nearly everyone had left town—I remember you went back to Indiana—so we just had John Johnson and his wife. After dinner, John was waxing philosophical about being head and about the search for the next head. I thought maybe he was contemplating his retirement. He said the most important thing was that the person should be 'called to service and not to power.' Something about that phrase…it stuck with me. Kent, too. I wasn't even sure I knew what he meant by it. But now I think I know what it means. It means Kay. Her calling is power."

Michael nodded. "And John's calling was service."

7

The doctor had suggested that Michael take two weeks off school after the surgery, but Michael felt he could return in one. To prepare for his absence, he taped four lectures for his philosophy class by sitting in the living room chair and speaking into a video camera he borrowed from school. For his other classes, he wrote out instructions for the substitute teacher.

The weekend before his surgery, Michael went for a five-mile run on Saturday morning. Li-Li, still on a hiatus from running, stayed at home. He spent Saturday afternoon doing yard work. Then he cleaned out the roof gutters; the rainy season would be starting soon. He took Li-Li to dinner in San Francisco on Saturday night. On Sunday morning he played a tennis match with his toughest competitor and won. Leanna observed that he seemed intent on cramming every activity of life into the two-day weekend. She was right: he was trying to squeeze the most of his last two days. In the depths of his mind he was terrified of his surgery. In that crazy part of the mind that harbors our worst fears, he believed he was going to die on the operating table.

For late Sunday afternoon he had scheduled with Leanna an outdoor photo shoot that he had wanted to do for months.

He wanted to collaborate with her to make something special, like their first shoot. He hadn't been in his darkroom since she moved in, and he missed it. The shoot would be in black and white of Li-Li nude on a hillside beside some beautifully formed dead trees, just before sunset, taking advantage of the long shadows cast by the low November sun. Her posing instruction was to become one of the trees. It would play to her strengths as a model.

Leanna was not in the mood to do the shoot. By the time they reached the site, she had complained about the long walk, fatigue, and the flies. It was one of her moods. She posed with such petulant body language that when Michael would view the contact sheets two weeks later, he would conclude that there was not a usable image among them.

Walking back, Michael looked up and saw a full autumn moon, rising huge and orange just above the hills in the darkening eastern horizon. Perhaps it was a good omen about his surgery.

"Oh, look, Li-Li," he said, hoping the beautiful sight might restore her mood. "See the moon."

She glanced at it and replied, "It's the color of baby shit."

8

On the morning of his surgery, Li-Li drove Michael to the hospital and sat with him in the waiting room until he was called. He gave Li-Li a last hug, and then he went into a pre-surgery room where he was shaved and dressed in a hospital gown. Then he had to wait for over an hour, plenty of time to let his imagination run wild. He might never wake up from the surgery (the consent form had made that possibility clear), or they could discover that the cancer had spread beyond the prostate. Both his parents had died of cancer, his best friend from high school had died of cancer in his early thirties, and even his boyhood dog had died of cancer. He imagined being swept away by a tide of bad cancer karma. He had always feared death, and he feared cancer in particular. For the past month he had used the activities of everyday life to push his fears to the back of his mind. Now they came crashing forward. He felt so terrified that his fingertips were numb.

There was an added dimension: Not only did he want to live, but also he did not want Li-Li to be left alone. She must be back at the lab by now. He imagined her in her white lab coat, gloves, and goggles, taking measurements and recording data on her laptop. He hoped she would not worry too much. It occurred to him that he was her only real friend in the states, and that she was now dependent upon him—emotionally and materially. If he were to die, she would be devastated. The thought of her having that experience was unbearable to him. His eyes welled up with tears. He hoped for a good outcome so intensely that he understood why people prayed. He wished he could wait on his redwood stump, talking to the baseball.

What he did instead was silently to tell himself his story as one might comfort a sick or frightened child with a favorite fairly tale. It was his own story of finding Li-Li, the woman who made sense of everything that had gone before. If his life were to end here, prematurely, the happiness of his story would be that he had found her; the tragedy would be that he would no longer be around to make her so happy she could cry. Whatever the outcome, it would be a story of love.

He awoke to a recovery room nurse saying his name. He was alive. He moved his hand beneath the blanket and felt himself. Sure enough, there was a catheter tube running into his penis. He must have still been sedated, for he noted it with clinical detachment. They wheeled him to his room, and when he was settled, he took out the photo of Li-Li he had brought with him and looked at it. Then he fell asleep.

Leanna's confidence about the outcome of his surgery had cracked when she walked out of the lab that afternoon. In a state of panic, she drove to the hospital far above the speed limit. When she walked into the room and saw him sleeping amid tubes, IV bottles, and monitors, she thought of an astronaut in a space capsule. She saw that her photo was on his bedside table, and she felt moved. She had brought Fungus, and she took him from her bag and put him beside her photo. When Michael awoke, she was on the far side of the room, gazing out the window. She came to his bedside and took his hand, careful not to disturb the IV tube. "I love you," she said.

Michael was allowed to go home the following afternoon. He had a catheter inside him and a urine bag strapped to his leg under loose-fitting sweatpants. He did not want Li-Li to see the catheter. There was something awful about it, and he wanted to protect her from the sight and to protect himself from the shame. Aside from occasional bladder spasms that froze him in his tracks, the post-surgical pain was milder than he had expected, more an abdominal soreness as if he had done a few hundred sit-ups. The psychological distress was worse—not only worrying about the lab results but also having something so primal as peeing now compromised by a plastic tube stuck in his penis. He felt debilitated and old. He felt unworthy of Li-Li.

In college one of Michael's favorite philosophers had been the French phenomenologist Merleau-Ponty. What Michael best remembered about him was his answer to the most fundamental question of life: what is our relation to the world? Merleau-Ponty's answer was embodied in the phrase, *je peux du monde*—literally, "I am able the world." We connect to the world by our active capacity—we can walk (or earlier, crawl), we can see, hear, and touch the world, throw a rock or a baseball, talk and sing, write poetry, grow food, discover molecules, make love, and build houses. We are what we can do. Life is good when our *je peux* feels strong; when our *je peux* weakens, life is descending. For Michael, his *je peux* had never felt so weak.

He said nothing of this to Li-Li. Clenching his fists, he plowed ahead. While Leanna was at work that week, he ventured out to the grocery store, his catheter and urine bag concealed under his sweat pants. He thought his face looked a little drawn, so in spite of a diminished appetite, he forced himself to eat plentiful amounts of healthy foods: fresh fruits and vegetables and high-quality protein. He drank lots of water (and emptied his urine bag frequently). Somehow wheat germ tasted especially good, so he had some every day as a mid-afternoon snack. Before Leanna came home, he carefully showered and put on a fresh shirt (and fresh sweat pants), and he made them nice dinners.

After the catheter was removed a week later, he passed only a small amount of urine voluntarily, the rest dripping like a leaky faucet into absorbent underwear liners he had to change every few hours. Overnight he had become a man who shops in the geriatric aisle of the drugstore.

During his first shower after the removal of the catheter, Michael soaped and gently stimulated his penis. Nothing happened. It might as well have been his index finger. His heart sank. The faucet for his urine was broken, and his penis had gone dead to the eroticism of the world. He had been mutilated, and his *je peux* was diminished. A sense of defeat spread through his body like poison. He felt like someone hanging to the edge of cliff by his weakening fingers, afraid to look down.

He made an effort to focus on the positive. He had grown up with the command "Count your blessings" as a moral imperative. It was one of his mother's favorite sayings. He also understood its therapeutic value. So count them he did. He had found Li-Li, his other half and the goal of his story, and she was sticking by him. He loved his teaching job and he owned a nice little house in the Berkeley hills, one of the better spots on the face of the earth. He was fit and otherwise in good health. Those were significant blessings.

When the lab report came back, it showed that the cancer, while extensive in his prostate, did not appear to have penetrated the capsule. No further treatment, neither radiation nor chemotherapy, was deemed necessary, and the surgeon was "cautiously optimistic" about his prognosis. His first blood test two weeks later was clean—another good sign. He had this, too, to be thankful for. He would be monitored with a blood test every six months for five years, once a year after that. Based on his PSA level before surgery and the lab analysis of his removed prostate after surgery, his chance of a cancer recurrence was 40%. With clean blood tests, the probability would steadily diminish over time.

Probability is a strong mixture of reality and unreality. If there are ten socks in a drawer and only four of them are red, our chances of reaching in blind and pulling out a red sock are 40%. But is 40% real? No, only the red or white sock we pull out is real. Right now, it is raining or it is not raining. That is real. Tomorrow's weather is at this moment not real. It is a thought in our minds, no more real that a flying elephant. But we cannot carry this skeptical thought experiment too far. If there is a 90% chance of rain, we carry our umbrellas. (And 90% of the time we're glad we did!)

Kierkegaard said that man lives forward and knows backward. Our interest in probability reveals our desire to peek, to skip ahead in a story and read the last chapter. Don't we sometimes say that the suspense is killing us? Michael did not want to look up those tables on the internet (which he did too often, as if they were going to be revised) and find the probability, which seemed ultimately unreal; rather, he wanted to *know* whether his cancer would return. Or so he thought. Actually, what Michael wanted to know was that his cancer would *not* return. He wanted a future without a red sock.

Michael had been raised with a strong work ethic, and one tenet of it was to make the most of what you have. He returned to school in a week. Throughout the day he did Kegel exercises, which he had started before the surgery, to help his urine control. He ate foods from the anti-cancer diet. He increased his daily walking until he was up to five miles a day, and as soon as he got the surgeon's okay, he resumed running and working out at the gym. His bladder control began to return.

At Christmas break, Michael dipped into his savings to treat them to a trip to Hawaii. Staying on Maui, they went for early morning runs along the ocean, Li-Li's first running since her meltdown on the trail that day the previous summer. They rented snorkeling gear and held hands as they swam like clumsy sea mammals gazing with wonder at exotic shells, brilliantly colored fish, and sea turtles. They took rainforest hikes and watched surfers on the north shore. Li-Li had put Fungus into her suitcase, so they had fun photographing him in various poses: sitting on the back of a motorcycle with the Hawaii license plate visible, on the balcony looking out over the ocean, having a staring match with a gecko that appeared on their bathroom wall, looking down on the clouds from Haleakala at 12,000 feet.

They played in the surf like puppies and sunned themselves at the nude beach to golden, all-over tans—hers darker than his—and the sight of his own tanned body in the mirror improved Michael's sense of well-being. They had sunset dinners on the patios of great restaurants. They took evening walks, luxuriating in the soft tropical breezes. Li-Li bought him a cigar, and one night he smoked it overlooking the beach, listening to the sweet soft roar of the waves while Li-Li leaned against his shoulder.

In the bedroom of their rented condo, Li-Li kissed him with love and desire, and they played on the bed in all the ways that he was able. They basked in the glow of their mutual love, and in spite of their obvious age difference, smiling people asked if they were on their honeymoon. Michael's bladder control was nearing 100%, and he felt healthy, loved by Li-Li, and blessed. His *je peux* was growing again.

Three months after the surgery, Michael still could not become fully erect. He visited an internet forum of prostate cancer patients and read heartwarming stories of wives who continued to be loving and sexual toward their husbands in spite of erectile problems. Some said it had brought them closer together and taught them that sex is more about intimacy and love than physical performance and pleasure. Though there were still plenty of sexual activities he and Li-Li could enjoy, she was not interested. She had not kissed him deeply since Hawaii. When he asked, she confessed that she had lost her feelings of passion for him, but she assured him that for her this was not a deal-breaker. She still loved him, still wanted to marry him, and still wanted to bring Mason or Chloe into their family.

Michael wistfully imagined how Marilyn would have reacted to his surgery, inventing new and exciting sexual activities for them. Sometimes he was worried by a voice in his head saying, "Are you crazy—you're going to marry a woman who no longer wants to have sex with you?" But he was wary of those destructive voices: you're too fat, you need to make more money, you should worry about what people think, your wife is a child, a marriage without good sex cannot be a good marriage. He thought of these as the voices of snakes, sneaky and venomous, capable of ruining a life, poisoning a story.

At many of the weddings he had shot, someone—often the officiant, but maybe a parent of the bride or groom during a toast—would remind the couple that the health of their marriage would depend not on the heat of romance but the warmth of friendship, care, mutual support, deep respect, patience, and generosity. Michael believed that he and Li-Li had all of those things. These voices, too, he heard in his head, and he thought of them as the voices of doves. He imagined their gentle cooing as the voices in his head that opposed the snakes. It was doves, not snakes, that he wanted to supply the voiceover for his story.

9

One afternoon Michael was watching a girls' soccer game after school and Kay stopped by the field. They stood together for a while, exchanging a few comments on the action. Looking over the field, Kay said, "I think the faculty is really embracing the 21st century education initiative."

"Really? Michael asked. His tone of skepticism was more evident than he had intended.

Kay snorted, "Well, I hope so."

A minute later, she added in a voice thick with maternal largesse, "Oh, I understand that it's hard for people to change. It's scary. I get that. That's why it's important to lean into discomfort."

Michael gazed across the field and said, "Well, the fact that someone choses not to change their class in a certain way—that doesn't mean they're afraid. It may just mean they think it's a bad idea."

One of the girls barely missed a goal and the small crowd—parents and friends of the players—gave a collective groan of sympathy followed by cheers of encouragement.

Kay turned to Michael. "If you look at our alums from the past few decades, you just don't see any CEOs, any top executives, any start-up founders. Especially among the girls.

That's what I'm trying to address." And she added with a short laugh, "—whether I'm getting much help or not."

Driving home, Michael came to a stop just before the bridge. There had been a wreck mid-span, so he resigned himself to a delay. He amused himself by imagining that people have no filter and whatever they think is automatically said aloud. He reimagined his conversation with Kay.

Kay: I want teachers to do what I tell them.

Michael: Teachers know better than you how to teach.

Kay: I'm right. I don't give a damn what they think. They would get with my program if they weren't afraid of change.

Michael: They not afraid. They're wise.

Kay: I want us to turn out people who get to the top of the ladder. That's our mission.

Michael: That's not our mission. Our mission is to broadly educate young people. I am in touch with a lot of my former students, and I feel very proud of them. They are doctors, heads of NGOs, teachers, lawyers, scientists, and engineers. Incidentally, you and my future mother-in-law would make a good pair.

Kay: You're one of the resisters, aren't you, you son-of-a-bitch?

Michael: You bet your sweet ass I am, you inhuman witch.

10

Leanna decided that she wanted them to get a puppy. Michael was not convinced. Having had a dog when he first moved to Berkeley, he wondered if Leanna knew how much work was involved. They were not like farms dogs that largely took care of themselves.

Li-Li surfed the internet reading up on breeds, and they made a few visits to the local shelters, walking down the rows as one dog backed away in fear, the next one growled, and the next wagged his tail and tried to put his nose through the fence. It made both their hearts bleed. Most were pit bull mixes, and none were puppies. They worried about what the dogs might have been through before they ended up in the shelter. They worried about their genes.

Then they visited a litter of purebred German Shepherds (Li-Li's preferred breed) at the home of a private breeder. When Michael looked into the mother's eyes, he had the uncanny sense that she wanted him to have one of her puppies. Li-Li was already playing with them. They picked out one of the females and then had to wait four weeks until she could leave the litter. It felt like the day would never come. Li-Li chose the name: Athena.

On the puppy's second day at their home, she crawled under the back fence and Michael and Leanna nearly had heart attacks before they found her. Until Michael could puppy-proof the fence, he took her to school with him every day where she was fawned over by the students. Everything in her new world was a tag-wagging delight (sticks, blowing leaves, Michael's socks as he tried to walk from room to room). In the coming weeks Athena grew rapidly, trained well, and dominated the other dogs in her puppy class. Though she bonded with both Li-Li and Michael, she chose Michael as her primary person. If Athena needed to go out in the middle of the night, she learned that he was the one to poke in the face with her muzzle. He took her on daily hikes (Li-Li was often too tired), and he practiced with her on obedience training. Li-Li slept much later than he did, so on Saturday mornings he took Athena to a training class, and when Li-Li awoke, they were back from the obedience lesson and Li-Li's favorite kind of beignet fresh from the bakery was waiting for her on the table.

Michael and Li-Li began to plan their wedding—or rather, Michael began to plan it. Li-Li typically came home from work exhausted, her experiments were not going well, and she had developed a sharp dislike for some of her co-workers. Though as svelte as ever, she became obsessed with her weight, and after every meal she went to her computer to record what she had eaten and calculate the calories. She complained about the small size about her breasts, and she seemed to be serious about getting a boob job some day. Michael waxed poetic about the exquisite charm of her small breasts, but it did not help. One night they went over to a restaurant in the city, but because Li-Li became irritated with some prankish teenage boys on the train, she descended into a rage and walked to the restaurant with her head down and her fists clenched. When they were seated, she refused to look at him. After one restaurant visit, Leanna felt she had eaten too much, and when she got home she made herself throw up. Michael heard her, and he made her promise she would never do it again.

Leanna started working out at the campus gym, using Michael's community membership card, swiping it at the turnstile at the entrance. One morning she was asked to show the card to an attendant, and since was obviously not "Michael," they confiscated the card and told her the real Michael would have to reclaim it. When Michael arrived home from school that afternoon, Leanna was in a rage, fuming at the attendant, at the unfairness of it all. She refused to eat dinner. Michael tried to calm her. He offered to buy her a membership (they were not expensive), but she wouldn't hear of it; she would never set foot in there again. When Michael stopped by the gym the next afternoon, they cheerfully returned his card with a reminder that only he could use it.

"See," he told Li-Li at home, "It was not a big deal. Let me get you your own membership."

But she was still enraged by the incident and the more reasonably and gently he tried to talk with her about it, the more upset she became, finally throwing herself on the bed crying and then refusing to be comforted. Michael felt the frightening loneliness of being unable to reach her.

Passing through the school library one afternoon, Michael paused at the new books display. After reading the back cover of a book on the latest brain research, he checked it out. That night he stayed up reading long after Li-Li had gone to bed. Recent research, aided by advances in brain imaging, had revealed the functions of the deep limbic system, the bonding and mood control center of the brain. He kept seeing Li-Li in the patients discussed, their feelings of worthlessness, their fits of anger, their bouts of low sexual desire, and their lack of empathy. Many had been helped by antidepressants. Though biased against the book's premise that depression was as much a physiological disease as diabetes or anemia, Michael ignored his own view in order to feel hope.

The next day, he told Leanna about the book and tried again to broach the subject of therapy. She said no.

"You've been trained as a scientist, for God's sake," he told her. "The case for you to see a therapist is overwhelming. If you had cancer, would you refuse to see a doctor?" The more reasonable his appeal, the angrier it made her.

In the months that Michael and Li-Li had lived together, he had realized that if mood is the weather of the mind, Li-Li's mind had a bad climate. Dark storms and frigid cold waves were quick to form and slow to dissipate. Small things prompted great storms, and she was frequently irritable and withdrawn (tiger, porcupine, jackrabbit, or tortoise).

A few weeks later, to Michael's surprise, Li-Li made an appointment with a psychiatrist, who diagnosed her with depression and put her on an anti-depressant. Within a week there was a noticeable change in climate. Her dark moments of self-loathing disappeared. Her mood swings were still present, but less pronounced. Her spurts of meanness toward others moderated.

Talk therapy was recommended to accompany drug therapy, so she agreed to try it. She hated the idea that she was paying someone money to listen to her talk about her problems. Isn't that what friends were for? And what was this woman supposed to do? She did not like being asked personal questions by a stranger; she felt pecked at, like the psychiatrist was a giant raptor trying with her sharp beak to break into Leanna's mind. She resented being asked how she felt when Ma sent her back to Singapore for high school; she didn't like to remember how she felt. Wasn't the point of therapy to make a person feel better, not worse? If you had bad memories, did it not make better sense to forget about them rather than to dredge them up? When the psychiatrist wasn't asking questions, she just sat there, making Leanna feel like she should come up with something. It felt so awkward that Leanna wanted to jump out of her skin. Sitting in the waiting room, she found herself hoping that no one would see her. She felt like she was losing face. After the third session she quit. If Michael thought therapists were so great, he could go to one himself.

Still, the tiny white pill taken once a day made a noticeable difference.

11

"Who are *you?*"

The caterpillar's question to Alice echoes throughout many stories and many lives. Alice wasn't sure how to answer because she had changed so much. The question of identity that had been an interesting intellectual puzzle for Michael in his grad school philosophy course had become a living nightmare during his breakup with Marilyn.

The day after her breakthrough therapy session in which she remembered her father's nighttime invasions of her girlhood bedroom, Marilyn called Michael at school but was unable to talk. Alarmed, he drove to her apartment, and when she opened her door, he was struck with horror. In the single strangest experience of his life, he felt to the core of his being that the person standing before him was not really Marilyn. Some deep part of her had been taken away. It was like a body snatchers movie come to life.

Trembling, tears streaming down her face, she would not let him in.

"I'm afraid," she said.

"Of me?" he asked.

"Of everybody."

After twenty minutes of conversation in her doorway, she closed and locked the door and returned to her bed where she spent the rest of the day curled in a fetal position crying. Michael drove home feeling the panic of a lost child.

Michael was desperate to help in any way he could, but Marilyn had panic attacks in his presence. In desperation he bought a huge stuffed bear and left it on her doorstep with a note: "If you can't see me now, I hope you will hug this bear and think of it as symbolic of all the love and care I have for you." She sent a one-sentence email thanking him. Later, they had some long, soulful conversations on the phone, but she would not, or could not, see him, and she would not let him back—into her apartment or into her heart. She went to stay with her sister for several months, and she replaced her incompetent therapist with a good one. Over the next several years she slowly recovered, but she was lost to Michael forever.

Whenever Michael saw a body snatchers movie advertised, he remembered the day Marilyn had appeared at her front door as a stranger. She had loved him deeply—of that he was sure. Whoever she was that day, she was not the same person, and the terror of her transformation frightened him to the depths of his soul. She had turned out to be a shape-shifter.

Something similar had happened years earlier when Michael's aunt was diagnosed with Alzheimer's disease. Michael had seen her on his visits to Indiana, once or twice a year, over the course of her disease, and at each visit he saw a marked change from his previous visit. On one visit she alluded to her recent dinner date with a national news anchor. On another visit she thought Michael was her own son. Then her sentences degenerated into nonsense phrases, then she stopped speaking entirely, and on Michael's last visit before her death, she just stared into space as if she saw nothing. Many months before her death, Michael felt she had ceased to be herself, and when his parents phoned to tell him that she had died, he had to stop himself from saying, "But she died a long time ago."

One day a couple of Michael's students had come into his classroom excitedly talking about their biology class of the previous period. They had learned that every cell in the body replaces itself, some in a matter of years, the epidermis every two weeks. One of them turned to Michael with a variation on Alice's question, "If every cell in the body changes, how are we still the same person?" Of course, here common sense becomes impatient with philosophy. Zeno may have proven that motion is impossible, but if we're walking down the street, why should we give a crap what Zeno said? But the philosopher does not seem so irrelevant if a family member's mind slowly evaporates like a puddle or the woman you love with all your heart one day opens her door and looks at you as a stranger. Marilyn had raised the caterpillar's question from a logical puzzle (how can Alice both change and remain the same?) to an existential nightmare. What if the person we love becomes someone else?

Several years back Michael's mother, ravaged by cancer, lost weight and became weaker, but she was still unmistakably his mother. Even when the morphine caused her to see things out of corner of her eye, she commented with lucidity, "Good God, I thought I saw a skunk going into the closet. That damn morphine is making me see things again." Her mind was always her own; whether well or gravely ill, whether reminding him which lawyer should handle her will or seeing morphine-induced visions, she was unwaveringly his mother. Her life constituted a firm answer to the caterpillar's question. She knew who she was, and she knew that she loved her son. Michael wanted a wife whose love for him would be that strong.

Leanna never said, "It's that damn depression making me making feel hostile and mean." She seemed always inside her own story, and her moods sometimes left Michael worrying about the caterpillar's question. To Michael, the tortoise, jackrabbit, porcupine, or tiger that Li-Li sometimes became were masks worn by one unchanging person whose center was soft and good. That was his story.

But what if he were wrong?

12

One Saturday Leanna went shopping for a wedding dress, Michael in tow. Though she knew fashion, bridal wear was a new area. Their first stop was Saks, where as soon as they entered, she again felt like a country mouse, and this time Michael's company did nothing to help. The salesperson, a woman not much older than herself, oozed a patronizing sympathy in the sort of sing-song voice that some use addressing a child. The translation was not lost on either Michael or Leanna—"Honey, we have nothing here you could ever afford."

Michael did his best to cheer her up. They went to lunch and then saw a matinee on the way home, a movie they both loved. To Michael's surprise, Li-Li shook off her treatment at Saks, and that evening she found online a simple and inexpensive ivory wedding dress, knee-length, and she decided to embellish it by having a silk sash with a bow in back sewn to the waist. They went to a seamstress to do the work. Michael decided to have a necktie made of the same fabric. Trying to explain her idea to the seamstress, Li-Li grew frustrated and cried, and Michael felt a pang in his heart as he realized how much Leanna needed her mother—or at least a girlfriend—at a time like this.

Their wedding was to be small, about twenty people. There would be dinner in a private room at a very good restaurant followed by a candlelight ceremony at a local church, and then cake and champagne at their home. Michael had put together the simple ceremony, and his friend Frank would officiate. Michael and Leanna planned the dinner menu at the restaurant. Leanna's mother and brother could not attend the wedding because of their immigration problems, and it seemed her father could not afford the flight. Leanna had invited several college friends, but none had committed. Michael began to worry that no one would be there for Li-Li, a thought that made his heart want to break. He felt like Nick Carraway trying to recruit attendees for Gatsby's funeral.

Michael was overjoyed when Li-Li's father changed his mind and decided to fly over from Singapore. Uncle would fly up from Texas, so that made two family members.

At last one of the invited college friends, Ellen, called to say she was coming. They could put her up in the cottage. Michael was relieved.

Two days before the wedding, Leanna picked up Pa at the airport and took him to lunch. Waiting for them to arrive, Michael paced the house, Athena at his heels. Michael was nearly as old as Leanna's father, and of a different race, culture, and country. It was not hard to imagine that Pa might dislike Michael. Leanna had never talked much about her father, and Michael did not know what to expect.

Within seconds of opening the door, Michael instinctively felt accepted. He and Pa shook hands as two men who were comrades in life. Michael and Leanna got Pa settled in the guest room, and they took him along on Athena's walks, cooked his favorite food (beefsteak) for dinner that night, and made sure he had access to the TV remote control. (He was something of a TV addict.) The next day Li-Li said it made her feel warm and fuzzy to see Michael and Pa getting along so well.

Uncle arrived, a little Chinese man of eighty with a strong Texas drawl and a twinkle in his eye, full of stories about his life and an abundance of entrepreneurial ideas wherever he looked. He believed there was a perfect spot for a donut shop a block from his hotel, and every time they saw him, he had completed more plans for it. Leanna's friend Ellen arrived, and Leanna took her to dinner while Michael dined with Pa and Uncle.

At the wedding dinner the mood was festive and happy. Uncle charmed everyone, and though Li-Li had worried that it would be an awkward event, she felt happy and at ease. Jennifer and Kent were there from school. Among Michael's friends an unspoken question hung in the air. "A forty year-old and a twenty-six year-old…are they crazy?" But there was also a rejoinder: "If anyone can do it, they can. They just might make this crazy thing work." The doves, not the snakes, had everyone's heart.

At the church, Ellen helped Leanna with her dress. The dress seemed too large through the bust, so Ellen helped Leanna stuff the cups with tissue. Because Li-Li did not want to break down in front of Ellen, she managed to control her frustrated sense of helplessness. As Ellen gushed about how beautiful and elegant she looked, Li-Li took a long look in the mirror and told herself that she liked what she saw.

Michael and Frank waited in a room just off the altar. The event was so momentous that Michael felt as if he were living in a dream. When it was time, they opened the door to a simple church bathed in the golden glow of candlelight. Frank and Michael walked to the altar, and the music started. Etta James' voice unraveled the words like honey, "At last…".

Leanna walked down the aisle alone, crying softly as she stepped onto the altar and took his hand. To Michael she seemed like a lost and lonely half seeking her other, and he felt the same way. His cow's udder full of love had someone to accept it; the soft catcher's mitt of his heart was open to receive her.

Just before they took their public vows, Li-Li and Mikey stepped to the back of the altar and in low voices exchanged private vows. He repeated his promise—an echo of the second arrow that pierced her heart—that he would stand by her and love her always. Li-Li had not really thought about what she would say, and she blurted out that she was the "most luckiest girl in the world." Though she would later feel humiliated by her blunder and not want to be reminded of it, its unpolished spontaneity touched Michael's heart.

Up at their house for a post-ceremony celebration, they served cake and opened champagne while Athena wagged her tail at the guests. Michael had shot dozens of wedding cake cuttings, and at most of them the bride and groom smooshed the icing on the other's face. When Michael and Li-Li fed each other a bite, they played it straight, no laughs at the other's expense. Michael took it as a good sign. Li-Li's father stepped forward to give the traditional Singaporean *Yam Sing*, the first syllable dawn out as long as possible. *Yaaaaaaaaam Sing*. The night was a high water mark of happiness in Michael's life story.

They took a short honeymoon to Mendocino, Athena in tow. They walked the quaint town, went canoeing, strolled the beaches, and watched movies in their cozy room. Athena, now a proud pre-adolescent, was savvy enough about the world to navigate its demands. She walked beside them without pulling on the leash, sniffed other dogs with politeness and restraint, sat in the canoe without trying to jump out, and lay patiently under the table while they ate. She ran with joyful abandon down the beach, barked at the water (she would not yet enter it), and chased sticks.

Walking down the street on their second morning there, Michael recognized a café where he and Marilyn had eaten lunch when she brought him to Mendocino years earlier and used her Tantric magic to give him the most ecstatic sexual experience of his life. Now he was with another woman, one whose happiness was his mission and to whom he had pledged that he would always be her faithful and caring husband. It was ironic that with this woman he had not had any sexual contact since they were in Hawaii six months ago. To Michael that meant that love can take many forms, many expressions, many ways of being lived. His regrets about his condition and their sex life notwithstanding, he was at peace with the love he and Li-Li shared. The doves were telling his story.

13

When the wheels of the plane touched the runway in Singapore, Li-Li started to cry. Michael took her hand. Unable to visit Singapore during the time she was awaiting her green card, Leanna had not been there in six years.

After clearing customs, they walked into the visitors' area where Ma and Pa were waiting to meet them. Li-Li threw her arms around her mother and burst into tears. Though Leanna and her mother had not seen each other for those six years, Ma remained dry eyed and looked embarrassed. Pa pumped Michael's hand like they were old friends. It was after midnight, so Pa drove them in his taxi to their small hotel.

On one of their first evenings in Singapore, Leanna and Michael went to a wedding celebration dinner, complete with tea ceremony, in the flat of Li-Li's maternal grandmother whom she called Por Por. A dozen or so relatives attended from Ma's side of the family, and many of the dishes were special family recipes.

Por Por had brought her children to Singapore from China after World War II, and she still spoke no English. Though English was the official language of Singapore, many older residents did not speak it. Por Por was ninety now, mostly toothless and frail, but she sat in her chair wearing her bedroom slippers and alertly watched the proceedings with matriarchal approval. Michael wanted to have a conversation with her, so he asked Ma to translate. He told Por Por that he would always take good care of Leanna. She told him with pride that she had taught all of her children to correctly use chopsticks, a remark Michael mulled over for some time to come. At the end of the conversation, Por Por smiled her toothless smile and gave Michael a kiss on the cheek and then a vigorous salute. He saluted back.

Michael found Singapore a modern metropolis with a gleaming downtown that made it seem like a boom city in the American sunbelt. Orchard Road was a high-end shopping mecca. Beyond the downtown stretched miles of seemingly identical high-rise apartment buildings built and administered by Singapore's Housing Development Board. Eighty-five percent of the population lived in these HDB buildings, and most owned, not rented, their apartments. It seemed like communist residential architecture with private ownership; they reminded him of the sterile apartment buildings he had seen in Poland. Uniform and soulless, surrounded by narrow strips of grass and skinny trees, these concrete monoliths did not look much different than those of densely populated intercity housing developments in the states, where the very architecture was sometimes blamed for the culture of drugs and crime. Here everyone seemed law-abiding and content, and nowhere could one see graffiti or even litter. Chewing gum was outlawed. Punishments for crimes were draconian. Over thirty crimes, including vandalism, carried sentences of caning in addition to jail time, and Singapore had the second highest per capita execution rate in the world. The massive HDB buildings were clustered into little satellite villages, each with its schools, shopping malls, and food courts where dishes were tasty and inexpensive. It all made practical sense.

There were a few condominiums in Singapore, more unique and upscale, seldom-realized symbols of affluence. Free-standing houses were so rare that after a week in Singapore, Michael still hadn't seen one.

Pa seemed content. He drove his cab, spent time with his buddies, rented out the rooms in his apartment so that six adults lived in what was basically a two-bedroom apartment. Ma owned her own small apartment in a newer building, and she seemed a little lonely. Back in Texas, Uncle was forever consulting an immigration attorney about how to expedite her return to the states, but Ma seemed resigned to never returning. Li-Li told Michael that Uncle was still in love with Ma. Nothing suggested that Ma felt the same. Her plan for herself and her two children to move up rungs in the ladder by becoming permanent U.S. residents had succeeded by only one-third. She did not hide her displeasure that Leanna was not pursuing her PhD. Though she seemed to think that Michael was too old for Leanna, his educated and gentlemanly demeanor and Pa's report on his nice home and his loving treatment of Leanna met with her approval.

Leanna and her friends talked a lot about eating and shopping—he was told these were the two greatest interests of Singaporeans—and gossip, but little about their work and nothing about national or world politics. A few of her friends were married and had babies, but most were still single, and they devoted a lot of their energy to nightlife–glitzy discos with events sponsored by a vodka label, baited with suggestive names like "threesome." Michael couldn't help thinking that Leanna's friends were still seeking a status of "cool" a decade after Michael's former students would have outgrown such a need—if they ever had it in the first place. Michael found it all depressingly Vegas, and he noted uneasily that Leanna's eyes lit up hearing about everything he found shallow. If there was any sort of counter-culture there, Michael saw no traces of it. He expressed none of this to Li-Li.

Because few Singaporean models would pose nude, and because Leanna was such a good model, the three shoots she had booked before the trip (enough to pay for one plane ticket) became nine, and Michael, to his chagrin, found himself spending entire days on his own.

On a day when Leanna had three photo shoots, she left their hotel early and would not be back until almost midnight. Michael wandered the city, shuffling through the sauna-like heat. He found the Singapore Art Museum where he had planned to spend the morning, but the museum, a converted school, consisted of only a few rooms of art. It was the dinkiest art museum he had ever seen. In less than an hour he had seen every work of art twice. Tour book in hand, he walked the city alone and in the late afternoon he found himself in a bar whose patrons were Caucasian expat men and young Singaporean women. He ordered a bourbon over ice and fell into a conversation with a middle-aged British man named Owen who was working in Singapore for an investment bank. Owen told Michael about the "five Cs," a well-known phrase used by Singaporeans themselves, with only a trace of irony, to identify their primary life-goals: cash, credit card, car, country club, and condominium. Owen did not mince words: Singaporeans were shallow and materialistic, and he couldn't wait to return to London. As for the curious mixture of young Asian women and middle-aged expats at the bar, Owen explained that Caucasian men were highly sought after by local women because they treated women so much better than did Singaporean men, for whom a wife was just a cook, baby-maker, and child-raiser. Though Michael found the Owen's cynicism off-putting, he wondered how true his description was. He left the bar feeling uneasy.

Though Leanna sensed that filling so many days with photo shoots was unfair to Michael, she could not resist the intoxication of being an instant star. When Li-Li brought Michael to social functions, she was at a loss for how to integrate him into her old friends or her family. It just wasn't a social skill she had ever learned. When they arrived at the tea ceremony for Pa's side of the family, she left him as soon as they walked in the door, and Michael spent the next two hours socializing as best he could with the people who spoke English. People were polite to Michael, but no one he met exhibited any curiosity about him or about the world outside their island city-state. Michael held up the conversations by asking them about themselves.

On the plane, he and Li-Li wrote thank you notes to all the relatives who had given wedding presents of red envelopes containing cash. The envelopes were given to Pa, who pocketed the money to pay for the wedding banquet. Li-Li said that was the practice. Michael and Li-Li did a couple of crossword puzzles together, and then she curled up against the window to sleep.

Michael had been disappointed in Singapore, though he realized the fault was partly his own. From his familiarity with Chinese cinema, Buddhism and Taoism, the *Tao Te Ching*, and Chinese poetry, he had expected something deeper, more colorful, more spiritual, and more soulful than what he found. Michael understood the dangers of ethnocentrism, how easy it was to take a quick glance at another culture and find it wanting, so he tried to temper his disappointment.

Michael looked at his sleeping wife. Having met Li-Li's mother, he thought about his own mother, and he wished deeply that she could have met Leanna. After Michael's father died, she returned to the job teaching Latin from which she had earlier retired. She played golf, walked five miles a day, and volunteered at the church. She visited him in Berkeley twice a year. Her lifelong vice of cigarette smoking finally caught up with her, and she was stricken with cancer. He visited her regularly during her decline, and he was able to get back to Indiana for the end.

The night he arrived she sank into what seemed like a coma. The hospice people had brought in a hospital bed and set it up in the den where, as a boy, he had played with his toys on the floor while his mother and father watched TV or read, and sometimes the three of them played cards or board games. Now his mother was dying in that same room, his father ten years gone. He held her hand, daubed cream on her parched lips. Later that night, over her previously impassive face there moved a look of deep and aching sadness. The hospice booklet said that hearing is the last sense to go, so he leaned close to her face and told her in a quaking voice that he loved her and that he knew she had always loved him, that she had been a wonderful mother and he hoped he had been a good son. Though she could not open her eyes, she moved her eyelids rapidly, and he knew she understood.

By the next morning her hands and feet turned cold, so he knew the end was near. A couple of hours later, her breathing slowed, and he saw her swallow—the first time in two days—twice, in rapid succession. Then she grimaced, as if her spirit were wrenching itself away from her body. She exhaled, and there were no more breaths. He said, "Goodbye, Mother," and hugged her still warm body. Then he wept.

His mother had met Marilyn and with her mother's intuition she sensed how deeply Marilyn loved Michael. She had been upset and perplexed when the relationship fell apart. The incest survivor syndrome was beyond her comprehension.

Now, from 35,000 feet above the Pacific, he wanted to tell her that he had found someone else, and that he was happy.

But was he happy?

Much of the time, yes, but their two weeks in Singapore gave him pause. Recalling his loneliest moments in Singapore, he allowed himself to hear the snakes saying that his marriage had been a terrible mistake. But beneath his frustration and disappointment there lay a bed of deep love, a sympathetic understanding of Li-Li's wounds, a sense of what the return to Singapore meant to her, and an understanding of the validation she received from modeling. He knew her childhood had left her needing a balm to soothe wounds that may never heal. He realized that only in the abstract could he understand the damage done by those dismissive junior high classmates in Texas, the college boys who did not notice her, a cold mother whose way of showing love—if that's what it was—consisted of prodding Leanna to climb the ladder. He remembered how his own mother had choked up every time he left her, and the image of Li-Li tearfully hugging her mother in the airport while her mother stood dried-eyed would stay with him forever. Besides, he was her husband, it was his mission to make her happy, and he had vowed to always stay with her. Commitment was what it meant to be a husband, and a husband was what he was now. It was the meaning of his story.

Her looked over at Li-Li. She was curled up in her seat, sleeping, and her blanket had slipped to the floor of the plane. He picked it up and gently lay it over her.

PART THREE:
TO HAVE AND TO HOLD

1

Back in Berkeley, Michael and Li-Li settled into married life. He taught. She worked at the lab. During the school year they took turns cooking, but in the summer he became a househusband, preparing dinner and then sitting on the front porch with Athena to wait for Li-Li's car to appear. He had some rose bushes in his back yard, so he often set a vase with a freshly cut rose or two on the table. After dinner, they would take a walk over to the Berkeley Rose Garden with Athena and watch the sunset, or they might take Athena to a nearby meadow and throw her rope toy for her. Li-Li would jump on Michael's back and he would trot after Athena. In the evening they would sit on the living room floor and play scrabble. She was by far the better player, though he sometimes amused her by making up joke words. Like *tsip*. When he placed the tiles on the board, she looked at him with schoolmarm disapproval. He explained, deadpan, "It's when one of those African flies takes a very tiny drink." She responded with a face palm and he fell over laughing.

One afternoon when Michael got home from school, he made a pot of spaghetti sauce and left it on the stove to simmer while he took Athena to run in the Berkeley hills. An early season rain had fallen the night before, so the air was clear.

When they reached the top of the hill, he could see San Francisco as if it were a block away. He paused a moment, jogging in place, while Athena sniffed a flat oval of grass where a deer had bedded down. Looking out at the city sparkling under a brilliant blue sky, Michael realized that he was happy.

The unsettling feelings from his visit to Singapore had been overpowered by the happy rhythm of daily life with Li-Li, the warmth of their home, and the pleasure of teaching in his classroom at school. Though he felt occasional moments of anxiety about the possible return of his cancer, he felt more strongly the gratitude of being well and alive in the present. The gentle cooing of the doves prevailed over the hissing of the snakes.

When Michael was a student at Indiana, one of his favorite novels was *The Great Gatsby*. It was now one of his favorite books to teach. He loved its wistful romanticism, Gatsby's yearning for something just beyond his reach, like a Tantalus whose torture of frustration is outweighed by the allure of expectation. Moved as Michael was by those sentiments, his feeling for Jay Gatsby was sympathy, not empathy. Michael was a romantic of a different sort. He was a romantic of the here and now, not the beyond. Whereas Gatsby yearned for the green light at the end of the dock, Michael did not want some enchanted light that Leanna represented. He just wanted Leanna. He wanted their evening walks, their games of scrabble, their shouts of "Collie" when they said the same word at the same time. He wanted the moments when he made her so happy she could cry. He wanted what he had—and nothing more. The romantic glow surrounded her like a nimbus—it did not lie beyond.

How did these two romantics of different kinds, Michael Taylor and Jay Gatsby, come about?

Jay Gatz, we remember, was a Midwestern boy whose life was too small for his restless soul. He worked hard—though he didn't know toward what—doing his calisthenics, studying electricity, and practicing elocution and poise. As a young soldier he fell in love with Daisy, an experience that included the feeling he could climb above it all and "suck on the pap of life." Later events, that he became wealthy and was murdered in his pool, were detail; the core of his story was the elusive dream he strove for.

Michael's quest was not to repeat the past, but to create something similar to it. He wanted to live in a warm nest like the one he had enjoyed as a boy. Michael's happiest childhood moments were playing with his toys on the floor of the den with the dog beside him while his mother and father sat in their chairs. If it were summer the music of the crickets and peepers could be heard through the open windows. In winter a gentle snow might be falling and his mother would make hot chocolate on the stove. Adult happiness for Michael was simply refinding these moments in a new form. Did Michael's original model of happiness make his current happiness a mere shadow? It did not. Quite the opposite, in fact. His original happiness added a layer of depth to his current happiness, like a cookie containing the taste of all the cookies eaten before.

Michael's romanticism was a happy blessing; Gatsby's was a beautiful curse. The stories of Michael Taylor and Jay Gatsby remind us that what makes us happy as adults is shaped by what made us happy or sad as children. As Freud said, money never makes adults happy because money was not what they wanted when they were children. Gatsby yearned for what he had never known; Michael desired what he had known well.

Leanna's quest was different. She, too, possessed happy memories of her childhood in Texas playing with her brother or watching Uncle make biscuits on a Sunday morning. But what shaped her were the bad memories, the moments of feeling unseen or unheard, moments of feeling diminished or abandoned. Now her quest was to be so seen and heard that the feeling would extend back into her childhood. When Nick reminded Gatsby that you can't repeat the past, Gatsby responded, "Of course you can." The English word *repeat* derives from the Latin *repetere,* meaning to seek again. *Petere* has a range of meanings from passive (to ask) to active (to pursue). Gatsby pursued Daisy. Li-Li pursued being seen and heard. It made her charmingly fearless (excited to jump from a plane, uninhibited about posing nude), because the strength of her pursuits trumped any risk (falling to one's death, feeling embarrassed). It also made her attractive to others. Passive whiners drive us crazy; active pursuers capture our admiration. It was why Nick liked Gatsby above all others. Daisy and Tom possessed; Gatsby pursued. Like Gatsby, Leanna had embarked on her own Ben Franklinesque list of self-improvements with determination. Though in Singapore she felt more comfortable, in America she felt more alive.

2

We give little thought to the hundreds of strangers we see every week, on the sidewalks, in the stores, on the commuter train. For one thing, there are too many of them. But sometimes our attention will light on someone, and if our thoughts go beyond the physical (what strange shoes those are, how does he keep his pants up?) what we often see is a story—short and spontaneously composed, but a story nonetheless. A cartoon drawn of the world might show storybooks with feet and legs boarding the commuter train, walking down sidewalks, dining in restaurants. We can't stop to read the other stories, so we guess them from the covers, or we ignore them entirely. We are a society of mostly closed books, leaving others to guess our stories.

Occasionally Michael felt the eyes of a storyteller fall on Li-Li and him, and it wasn't hard to imagine the narrative the person was constructing: a middle-aged Caucasian man, well-dressed, and a pretty Asia woman who looked young enough to be his daughter wearing a wedding ring—a *quid pro quo* marriage, hot sex and a trophy wife for him, financial security and perhaps U.S. citizenship for her. Sometimes the storyteller—especially if a middle-aged women—wore an undisguised look of condemnation. Once he thought he heard a woman actually say, "Harumph." He was too dumbstruck to laugh—or to flip her off. Sometimes from a woman in her twenties, it was a look of curious interest. A man Michael's age might exude a conspiratorial sympathy.

When Michael received a couple of inquiries about shooting summer weddings, he gave it some thought. He liked shooting weddings. He liked the fly-on-the-wall voyeurism of watching the nervous excitement of the day. He liked being a panther on the prowl for moments that could become photographic works of art. His favorite shots were black and white candids of the bride getting ready, detail shots of the table setting, the cake, the rings. He liked to capture that moment when the bride and groom were holding hands, a close-up black and white with a wide open aperture so the hands were in tack-sharp focus and the background softly blurred. He lived for those moments when, weeks later, the bride—and once the groom—got teary-eyed seeing the prints that he had made and toned in his darkroom like an old world craftsman. (He was making the bride so happy she could cry.) But shooting a wedding consumed the whole weekend, not to mention the many hours of work afterwards. After his relationship with Marilyn had ended, work—both photography and teaching—had become something of a balm for his wounded soul. In five years he had managed to pay for his cameras and darkroom. But now he wanted to balance teaching with his time as a husband. He would rather spend weekends with Li-Li than shooting a wedding. With nostalgic regret, he decided to shoot no more weddings. He emailed the wedding planners he had worked with and he took down his website.

With his summers free, Michael started thinking about something that had piqued his interest a few years ago when he had been at a party with Marilyn and met a man who taught at San Quentin Prison. Remembering that now, he found the organization's website and a few weeks later attended an orientation session. He walked out convinced he wanted to do it.

He signed on as a tutor for the spring term, once a week on Thursday evenings. Though the ritual of entering the prison would eventually become routine, his first time felt as strange as landing on the moon. He checked in at the outside gate with his driver's license. The group of volunteers, escorted in by one of the permanent staff, walked down a sidewalk with administrative buildings on the right and San Francisco Bay to the left, the setting sun glittering on the water. When they reached the inner gate, they showed their ID's again, stood with arms outstretched to be checked with a metal-detecting wand, and then received an ultraviolet ink stamp on the wrist. A steel barred door opened, and they entered what seemed like a small cattle pen. The door closed behind them with a clang and the locking bolt shut with a loud crack. A guard behind inch-thick bullet-proof glass opened the steel barred door at the other end, and they entered the prison grounds.

The first sight was pleasant enough. They walked past the chapel, a long, low Spanish-style building with a well-tended rose garden in front. They started down an asphalt road that wound around the hospital to the exercise yard. Now it looked like prison. Men in blue, loose-fitting prison uniforms were milling about in a large blacktopped area that looked like a run-down urban playground. A group was playing basketball on a goal with no net. Some sat playing cards. Two men were playing chess at a steel picnic table bolted to a concrete base. One man was using an outdoor urinal. A few were doing pushups on the asphalt. Another was beating up a punching bag. Some were walking or jogging the perimeter. The exercise yard was separated from the education building and from the cell blocks by a tall chain link fence topped with spirals of razor wire. The outer boundary of this world was an ocher wall, forty feet high, topped with catwalks for the guards. At intervals, towers were manned by sharpshooters with high-powered rifles.

Walking toward the wooden ramshackle education building, Michael noticed geese scratching on the baseball field. They flew in and out at will, a freedom that mocked the confinement of the inmates. By the time Michael signed in at the education building, he felt so alien that he wished he could leave.

In the study hall, one of the tutors wrote a sign-up list on the blackboard with chalk. Michael's school used whiteboards and markers; he realized that he hadn't held a piece of chalk in twenty years. Michael was one of four tutors that evening, two in math and two in writing. The inmates began to drift in and sign up for one of the twenty-minute slots. Michael's first tutee, Teddy, was a student in the pre-college writing class. He was black man of about thirty with dreadlocks and an aura of reluctance, Michael sensed, about being tutored. His assignment was to write a personal essay about a physical object that had been important in his life, and he was stumped.

Michael asked him questions to help him find an object, and at last Teddy mentioned the gun. As a teenager he had begun selling drugs, and he once traded a large bag of dope for a handgun. The gun was loaded, and he kept it hidden in his room. Halfway between his home and school there was a young white woman known to do sexual massage out of her apartment, and the men who came and went were mostly white or Asian, often driving expensive cars. Teddy thought they would be an easy mark. Though he had done plenty of shoplifting and a few residential burglaries, he had never robbed anyone, but how hard could it be? He would stop a John on his way in; that way he would have at least the cash for the masseuse and probably more.

One day he put the gun in the big pocket of an army jacket and walked up and down the block until a man pulled up in a Lexus. He was an Asian man wearing a suit. Teddy stepped in front of him, put the gun to his stomach, and told him to hand over his wallet. Teddy's finger was on the trigger. Maybe his hand was shaking. The gun fired and the bullet blew a hole in the man's chest. Teddy ran two blocks with the gun still in his hand and was stopped by a squad car. His victim was dead before the ambulance arrived. Though Teddy was seventeen, he was tried as an adult. His claim that he had not meant to pull the trigger was not believed, and he was convicted of first-degree murder. That was fourteen years ago. His sentence was thirty-five to life.

There was a long silence. He had told the story as if it had happened to someone else.

"Do you remember what the gun looked like?" Michael asked.

"I can close my eyes and see it now. But I can't remember the man's face. I don't even know if I looked at it."

"Well, you could write your essay about the gun."

Teddy had a blank sheet of paper in front of him. He held a yellow pencil in his hand. He looked defeated.

"What do you remember about it?" Michael asked.

"It was *loud*, man. I remember that. I thought it had exploded. That's about it, though." He put the pencil down.

"Think about when you were younger than seventeen. Any things come to mind?"

Michael thought of Fungus, his boyhood stuffed elephant that he and Li-Li had such fun with.

Teddy looked up. "I had a bicycle." He began to tell about his bike, a red banana-seat bike. A neighbor helped him alter the gear so that he tripled its speed, and he became the legend of his neighborhood, several times outrunning gangs of boys trying to steal it. He kept it in his room beside his bed. He gave it a name: Red Rover. As he told the story, his eyes brightened and his face lit up.

When he finished, Michael looked at him and said, "The story you just told me—that's your essay. Go write it down."

"Really?"

"Really," Michael answered. "That's your story. It's a good one."

Teddy frowned for a moment, and then his face softened into a smile. "Yeah," he said. "You're right. That's my story." He stood up. "Thanks, man."

Driving home, Michael couldn't wait to tell Li-Li all about it his evening, and the story of Teddy's bike was what he was going to tell her first.

3

Li-Li entertained him with funny ways of walking through the house, making crazy faces, barking like a dog when she heard him at the door. When she was in a good mood, she radiated a charm that lit up a room. Sometimes she crawled into the study in imitation of Athena and jumped into his lap. When they went to bed, he would read to her—short stories he thought she would like, novels at the rate of a chapter per night. Sometimes she read to him. She was a crossword *aficionado*, and they often did them together. Michael regularly filched the crossword page from his school's copy of the *New York Times* to bring home to her. For every five words she knew he might know one (usually from literature, politics, or older pop songs), and since those were words she was less likely to know, they made a good team. He thought it emblematic of their marriage, a union of complimentary differences. He left her love notes, wrote haiku and emailed them to her at work. She organized monthly cooking competitions, where the chef for the night had to invent a meal from a basket of ingredients chosen by the other. They ate in a nice restaurant once a month and wrote their respective reviews in a journal. They went on dates to the movies or ballet. When her lab held a pizza and movie night, and Michael always went and brought Athena.

Leanna had ever-changing favorite food items—a certain brand of rice crackers, dried plums from the Chinese food store, her favorite cereal—and Michael frequently brought them home, placing them in the pantry with Fungus standing proudly next to the package. Nothing made Leanna feel as happily loved as Michael's attention to her quirky likes. They developed a secret "I love you" signal, the palm placed over the heart, which they exchanged on special occasions in public or around the house when they felt a "love wave."

Sometimes after dinner, one of them would say, "Gee, Brain, what do you want to do tonight?" and the other would answer, "The same thing we do every night, Pinky—try to take over the world." The ritual had been started by Leanna (Michael was too old to have watched the animated TV series from which it came), and one night Michael remembered something his parents used to say when he was a boy. His father would sigh and say, "A farmer works 'till dusk from dawn," and his mother would respond, "but a woman's work is never done." Then they would both laugh. In this, too, Michael felt he and Li-Li were recreating happy memories of his boyhood house in Indiana.

Now that they had a dog, the only thing Michael wanted to add was Chloe or Mason, but Li-Li seemed not ready and he did not want to pressure her. When she felt the time was right, she would let him know.

Leanna had no real friends in Berkeley, and she had not connected closely with anyone at work. Michael knew she missed her undergraduate friends, now scattered about the country, as well as her friends in Singapore, so whenever she wanted to go shopping, he went along, trying to be girlfriend as well as husband. He went not grudgingly, but willingly, even enthusiastically. He liked watching her browse the clothes. Sometimes they took Athena along.

When Leanna asked his opinion on a skirt or a top, he gave it. Sometimes he called her attention to clothes he thought she'd like. Having done some fashion photography, he had a better eye for women's clothes than the average man, and he proved to be a good style bloodhound. When he carried her packages, she joked that he was her cabana boy. Now that she had a regular paycheck, she made some contribution to their household expenses, paid on her student load, and still had a nice chunk left each month for shopping. Her bargain staples (Old Navy and Forever 21) gave way to Banana Republic, J. Crew, and small, moderately-priced boutiques scattered around San Francisco. She was also becoming a connoisseur of makeup, so no shopping trip was complete without stopping at a makeup store or two. When they arrived home, she would model what she had bought, posing and twirling in front of the mirror.

"Are you sure you don't mind?" she asked him about going along on these shopping trips. "I love you so much," he answered, "that I am happy doing anything with you." It was not flattery—it was the truth. It is natural that we delight in watching those we love; one might even say it is a test.

One Saturday at breakfast Michael unfolded the paper, and when his eyes fell on the date, he was taken aback. It was the anniversary of his mother's death. He realized that he was wearing a shirt she had given him on what was her last Christmas. Too weak to shop, she had ordered several presents for him through the mail, a sweater and a couple of nice shirts. The memory of her determination that he have Christmas presents hit him like a train and his eyes filled with tears that spilled in rivulets onto his cheeks. Shocked, Leanna asked what was wrong. He cleared his throat and told her. After a brief pause, she said, "What do you want to have for dinner tonight?"

Michael was first stunned, and then angered. He wiped his eyes and kept his head down, pretending to be absorbed in the paper. Li-Li returned to doing her crossword. When he finished his coffee, he took Athena for a hike, thinking about Leanna's callous response—or lack of response. When he and Athena returned, he tried again, telling Li-Li the story of the Christmas presents and how much he still missed his mother. When he finished, there was a long pause, and then Li-Li said, "I don't know what to say."

She meant it literally, and Michael was moved by her poignant honesty. He thought again of the scene with Ma at the Singapore airport when Li-Li burst into tears and Ma gave her a short, stiff hug. It all made sense. The ways we comfort others when they are distressed or sad—whether through empathy, attempts at humor, or diversion—are at least partly learned. For Leanna, giving emotional comfort was a challenge akin to Michael being asked to make plumbing repairs—he had only the most rudimentary know-how, and for that reason he avoided them in any way he could. His anger melted into sympathy. At the moment she had said, "I don't know what to say," she had looked so vulnerable that his heart bled for her.

Being a good marriage partner requires skills, like cooking or carpentry, and he understood that Leanna was just learning. On his birthday of the first summer they were married, Leanna did done nothing in observance—no present, no special dinner, and not even a card. He hid his hurt and disappointment as expertly as a poker player with an empty hand. It was not mentioned until months later when Leanna remembered it with self-recrimination.

"I didn't even get you a present," she murmured.

"That's okay, Li-Li," he said.

"No, it isn't okay," she responded.

But it would be the last birthday she would ignore.

Li-Li liked to have projects, and Michael took a delight in observing her energetic commitment to them. She found a website where women traded cosmetics, and she daily engaged in arranging swaps of eye shadow, mascara, lipstick, and blush. She read up on cosmetics and became as knowledgeable as a wine connoisseur. Michael gently teased her that they may have to add on to the house to accommodate her growing supply. He recognized an entrepreneurial spirit in Li-Li that he admired.

One day Michael got a call at school. It was Li-Li, on the verge of tears. It was time for lunch, and she had opened her purse to find she had forgotten her wallet and had no money to go out for lunch. Michael paused and then said in an upbeat voice that she should ask someone to borrow a few dollars.

"I'd lose face," Li-Li said, her voice quaking.

"Just make a joke out of it," Michael said. "Say that otherwise you'll have to panhandle in front of the lab. Or ask the HR person. She can loan it to you out of petty cash. Really, it will be okay."

When Michael hung up the phone, he paused. The chorus of snakes said, "Lunch money! Jesus Christ, Michael. You married a child!"

That afternoon, he walked into the back yard to cut some roses for the dinner table, and then he wandered over to the redwood stump and sat down. Athena followed him, and when he took the baseball from the earthquake can, she sat expectantly while he turned it in his fingers. He said aloud, as if he were channeling one of the doves, "We're all children. For our whole lives, we carry in us the child we used to be. We either know and accept the inner child in ourselves and others, or we don't. And if we don't, we're less human, less real." Then he looked at Athena and said, "*The inner child*—Jesus. That sounds like California psychobabble, I know, but it's the truth."

How could he *not* love someone who was on the verge of tears for forgetting her lunch money? Of course, this was a rhetorical question for Michael, but not for everyone. For some, nothing kills love as surely as the discovery of weakness in the beloved. It is commonly assumed that we love others for their virtues. While Michael admired Li-Li's virtues, they were not what had pierced his heart. He loved her the most when she was being neither jackrabbit, porcupine, tortoise, nor tiger. He loved her most when her heart showed itself, even when it was the heart of a child. He could picture her as a skinny eight year-old in Texas, tightly clutching her lunch money, and something about the very image made him want to weep from love. He put away the baseball and returned to the house just as she came in from work. He hugged her, feeling as if his heart would burst through his chest. When she bent over to greet Athena, Li-Li did not see him wipe his eyes.

4

One day at school, Fontaine, the drama teacher, stopped Michael on campus and asked him to take a walk up the trail into the Redwoods. He was putting on a modern adaptation of *Lysistrada* for the fall drama production, and after reading the script, Kay Axelrod had called him in and blew her temper. The first thing out of her mouth was, "I'm so fucking pissed at you!" She said that the script was inappropriate for high school, and that his poor judgment raised questions about whether he was a good fit for the school.

"Jesus Christ—'a good fit'?" Michael exclaimed.

"I don't know," Fontaine said. "Should I be worried about my job?"

"How can you be worried about your job? You're an institution here. And how can she question whether you're a good fit. Some of us wonder whether *she's* a good fit for the school. "

Fontaine had taught at the school for over twenty years, one of John Johnson's first hires. He had grown up in Georgia, and he spoke with a Southern drawl in a booming baritone. He was a talented drama teacher with an instinctive ability to draw students out and to instill confidence in them, to motivate them to stretch, grow, and change. He was the only out gay person on the staff, and he provided a welcoming beacon for the students who were gay or thought they might be—or for those who were just geeky or weird. His magic with students was to exude an assurance that whoever they were, they were okay. Sometimes in the first few weeks of the term a student—usually a boy—might find Fontaine too overtly gay, or feel uncomfortable when he raised the pitch of this voice and played a female character as if it were his own skin, but in the end students were won over by his nurturing warmth and care and his unapologetic authenticity.

What neither Fontaine nor Michael knew at this time was the backstory of Kay's outburst. One of the school's most significant donors was a real estate developer whose wealth was in the hundreds of millions. Early in the last century, his family had owned thousands of undeveloped acres that was now some of Marin County's most prime real estate. His daughter Emily, who had ADD and whose mind was creative, brilliant, undisciplined, and disordered, was exploring her emerging sexuality and feeling more lesbian than straight. She was doing fairly well at the school thanks to a team of tutors, psychologists, and learning specialists wryly referred to by her teachers as Team Emily. The father, a conservative Catholic, was distressed about his daughter's sexual leanings, and he blamed Fontaine. He felt revolted by Fontaine's flamboyant, effeminate manner, his gushy energy, the colorful scarves he wore around his neck. His daughter talked about Fontaine in glowing terms, and he was sure her own flirtation with sexual perversion was an attempt to mimic Fontaine. He felt convinced that Fontaine encouraged it. He had expressed his concerns about Fontaine's influence more than once to Kay. He listened to Emily practicing her lines to *Lysistrada* with one of her friends—he became ever vigilant now when her friends were over—and heard references to vaginas and penises. It was not just the lines that enraged him, but that his daughter thought they were funny and laughed derisively at his objections. He hadn't spent thirty years working his way up the *Forbes* list of the wealthiest Americans to be made a fool of by a faggot school teacher who made less than his gardener. Or, to rephrase his objections—as rephrase them he did to Kay—he was not single-handedly doubling the school's endowment to have his daughter's mind screwed with at her most vulnerable age.

5

Clyde, the pet snake that Leanna had brought along when she moved in, needed to be fed about every three weeks, so Leanna or Michael would stop at the vivarium for a baby mouse. Leanna watched with keen interest as Clyde slowly sensed the mouse and began to move toward it. The mouse was quicker and sometimes scampered up to the snake, jumped over it, and once stepped on its nose. But finally, in a lightning move too fast to be followed with the human eye, the snake caught the mouse in his mouth and coiled around it, squeezing it to death. Then began the deliberate process of Clyde opening his mouth and slowly swallowing the mouse.

Michael watched the event, but with a different attitude than Leanna. While she watched with delight, Michael did not like it. Michael was not afflicted with the blinders to reality that some animal sympathizers have. After all, he had grown up on a farm. He knew the cycle of nature, and he had eaten pot roasts that months earlier had grazed a hundred yards from his bedroom window. But whenever Leanna plopped a mouse into Clyde's cage, his sympathies were with the mouse, and when it struggled against the greater power of the snake coiled around it, its eyes bulging, Michael felt sad for the mouse; he wanted it to escape and live.

Once Michael got his wish. For reasons unknown, Clyde did not approach the mouse. The next morning the mouse was still scampering around the cage, no doubt frantically searching for food. Leanna said that if that much time had passed, the snake would never take the mouse. Michael and Li-Li looked at one another; what were they to do?

"Keep him," they said simultaneously, and then they laughed and shouted, "Collie!" They fed the mouse a piece of bread, and it freely drank some of Clyde's water. Michael drove to the pet store and returned with a mouse house complete with a running wheel, cedar shavings, and food. The mouse, whom they named Mouse, became a pet.

Mouse grew up tame enough to be handled, and they bought him a large plastic ball with air holes that he played in, rolling it through the house. Athena watched with keen interest, her ears pointed. One night they decided to introduce Mouse and Athena, and they firmly instructed Athena not to pick him up in her mouth. Mouse crawled around on Athena, and when Athena could no longer contain herself, she gave Mouse two generous licks that left him as soaking wet as if he'd gone through a car wash. When Mouse recovered from the shock, he shook himself with indignity and furiously began grooming himself as Athena watched with a cocked head. Michael and Li-Li rolled on the floor with laughter.

6

One Sunday morning in October, Michael and Li-Li made their "Sunday breakfast." She whipped up pecan pancakes while he sliced melons, squeezed grapefruit and orange juice (a mixture of half of each was their preferred drink), and made scrambled eggs with scallions and parmesan. He read the editorial pages and the book review section of the paper while she combed the comics and the fashion section. They both read the food pages. After finishing their coffee, they went for a walk in the Berkeley hills. A hot, dry off-shore wind—the kind that occurred a couple of times a year in early autumn—was blowing so hard it made their faces sting and their eyes burn. It was a wind that blows down from the mountains, gaining in heat and velocity, until it hits the Bay Area like a blast from a furnace. Li-Li said the wind was giving her a headache. Feeling defeated and out-of-sorts, they turned back.

Driving home, they saw a distant plume of gray smoke rising across the bay in Marin County. Michael turned on the radio and heard that the hills above his school were on fire, the winds whipping the flames out of control. Already several homes had burned.

Back home, Li-Li went out grocery shopping and Michael sat beside the radio listening to the all-news station, which was now devoting non-stop coverage to the fire. Two dozen homes had been destroyed and more were threatened. Michael drank a glass of water. He had felt dehydrated all morning. The radio reported that the fire had jumped a highway, and the fire department had issued a mutual aid call. An evacuation order had been issued for a number of neighborhoods. Michael recognized some of the street names. The fire was burning its way toward his school. The radio announcer used a new term: *firestorm.*

Michael decided to call Andy, the head of buildings and grounds. His wife answered the phone and frantically told him that Andy had driven over to the campus. She implored Michael to make him return home; when Michael reminded her that he was calling from Berkeley, she seemed to ignore the fact.

Listening to the radio, Michael paced the house and drank another glass of water. Walking onto the deck and peering westward, he squinted toward a spreading cloud of ever darker smoke in the west. As he watched, he did not know that in the deeper recesses of his mind he was deciding to drive to the school, a decision (he did not realize this, either) that emanated from the incident of the newborn calf. It happened when he was seven.

One afternoon in the middle of calving season, Michael had just been let off the school bus and was walking up the lane to his house when he saw one of the cows in the corner of the lot. Her knew her; she was one of the young cows, about to have her first calf. She was standing awkwardly beside the fence, her legs splayed, facing the lane. When Michael got closer, he saw hanging from her vulva the front end of a baby calf, wrapped in the placenta like a raw chicken in a plastic bag. It twisted like a pinwheel, struggling to get free.

The cow bellowed plaintively. Michael froze in place. He had seen calf births, and they both frightened and fascinated him, but they were not like this. The cow had always been lying down, and the calf had barely moved until it was on the ground and the mother licked it clean. Why was this cow standing? She was looking at him. She seemed to be bellowing for help.

Michael ran. He ran from the cow, from his confusion, and from the boy who knew he should act but was paralyzed. He ran because it was the only way not to remain frozen.

When he got to the house, his mother was in the kitchen. She looked at him and said, "Goodness, Honey. You're all flushed. Did you run home? Are you sick?"

No, he said, he was all right, and he ran off to do his chores. He filled the hogs' water trough with the hose and, his hands trembling, fed the chickens. The image of the pin-wheeling calf, jerking in its filmy sack and half stuck in its mother, would not leave his mind. He thought he could hear the cow bellowing. When he walked behind the hen house, the ground started to spin and he bent over at the waist and threw up. He covered the vomit with dirt, wiped his mouth and chin on some leaves, and went to his room.

Later, when his father sat down at the supper table, he said grim-faced, "Well, we lost a calf."

"Oh, no." his mother said. "What happened?"

"It was that young cow. She went off to the lower lot to calve, and the calf suffocated. The placenta was still around its head. It was the heifer's first—couldn't figure out what to do, I guess."

"Is the cow okay"? his mother asked.

"She seems to be. I called the vet. But we lost that calf."

Michael wanted to ask about the calf being stuck, and why the heifer was standing, but the distance between the thinking the thoughts and forming the words was as far as the moon. He couldn't eat his supper, and his mother checked his temperature and put him to bed. When she left the room, he took from his bookshelf the coloring book they had given him at Sunday school, and he worked to color in all of the bible scenes. He knew it wouldn't make up for his running away, but he did it anyway. He kept seeing the cow and its half-born calf struggling for life.

People are not effects, determined by causes. From A, X might follow, but also might Y or Z. From Michael's afternoon of childhood trauma, he might have become a vegetarian or developed lactose intolerance. He might have become an inveterate bystander, quick to freeze in a crisis. Instead, his guilt hardened into a vow. There formed in the deepest part of him a stubborn resolve: He would never run away again.

Over the years, the cow in distress had returned in various forms, and now, decades later, it returned as a fire. He was not about to run. Did he realize the connection? He did not. The batter about to swing at the ball does not stop to wonder why he plays the game, what childhood decisions brought him to the baseball field rather than to the piano bench or the basketball court. In this moment, without asking why. Michael became focused and methodical. He changed into jeans and a long-sleeve shirt. He stuffed a t-shirt into his back pocket. He thought to remove his contacts and put on his glasses. He pulled on his baseball cap. He filled Athena's water dish. After writing Li-Li a note, he drove across the bridge to his school. Looking out over the water, it occurred to him that anything could happen in the hours to come.

A half-mile from the school, Michael realized that his was the only car heading toward the fire. All of the other cars, some with belongings tied to their roofs, were driving toward him. The evacuation area had been expanded. He was stopped by a police roadblock, where an grim-faced officer motioned him to turn around. Suppressing a retrograde urge to speed back to Berkeley and find a matinee to watch with Li-Li, he steered his car into a supermarket parking lot, locked it, and trotted to a nearby trailhead. Having helped with the cross-country team for several seasons, he knew the network of trails above the town like the back of his hand. This one would take him directly to the campus.

He ran the trail for a while, and when he began to feel the scratch of the smoke in the back of his throat, he slowed to a jog. The sunlight dimmed and took on an eerie tobacco-colored tint. Though it was just past noon, it seemed like dusk— or the end of the world. Sirens wailed, but they sounded far away. He tasted smoke on his tongue. He pulled the t-shirt from his back pocket and tied it around his face.

When he reached a clearing at the top of a hill, he stopped, dumbstruck. He saw an inferno. A wall of flames, taller than a house, burned halfway down the next hill in a ragged line like the unruly charge of an army. He heard a dull roar punctuated by sounds of cracking and snapping. Through the flames he saw the silhouette of a home, fully engulfed, and he heard the distant squawk of a smoke alarm. He felt like one of those tiny, ant-like figures in a Chinese landscape painting, dwarfed by the immense world of waterfalls, mountains, and sky—except that here the world was made of fire. Above his head, the sun was a pale brown disc.

For a moment Michael felt he might take flight, as if he were standing on the legs of a doe smelling smoke. The boy who would never again abandon that cow thought of Andy down there. He thought of the school. He felt a determination well up, his legs became his own, and he ran down the trail, through a last redwood grove, and emerged onto the campus lawn like a runner breaking the tape at the finish line.

Andy, holding a fire extinguisher, used his free hand to grab Michael by the shoulder and give him a vigorous shake, as if they were on a football field and Michael had just scored a go-ahead touchdown. Michael looked over the campus and saw six students, three boys and three girls, strategically positioned with garden hoses. The lawn sprinklers were on, lazily spinning spirals of water onto the grass. Bits of glowing ash and smoking embers were falling, and the students quickly doused them with the hoses.

The students saw Michael and waved.

One of the boys shouted, "We like the look, Mr. Taylor." Michael had not realized his t-shirt was still tied around his face.

"Thought I might hold up a liquor store on the way home," Michael called back.

About a dozen students had been on campus building a set for the fall drama production when a police cruiser drove by ordering an evacuation on its loudspeaker. Half of the students had gone home, but six, over Andy's objection, had chosen to stay. Andy had turned on the lawn sprinklers and the students had collected garden hoses from the maintenance shed and attached them to spigots. They had gathered all of the fire extinguishers on campus and carried them to the stone patio in front of the library. Andy had thought of making the students leave, but he was afraid that by that time driving out would be more dangerous than staying.

Andy explained the battle plan to Michael. Since the strong winds were blowing from the east, that direction was their worry. The eastern side of the campus was bordered by a road, and between the road and the school's buildings was a green lawn irrigated by sprinklers.

"When the fire gets here it won't burn the lawn," Andy said, "especially now that it's wet. So mostly what we have to do is watch for sparks and embers so they don't set the buildings on fire—the wood decking especially—or the roofs and the trees. A lot of the buildings are so close that if one goes, they all go." He thought that if worse came to worse and the campus burned, they could retreat to the middle of the soccer field where he had turned on the sprinklers.

"I think we'd be safe there," Andy said.

Michael took up a garden hose beside the live oak tree just off the patio of the library.

When the wooded hillside across the road begin to burn from the bottom toward the top, and the sound of roaring flames and cracking trees grew louder. There were three houses on this road, and he watched each catch fire and become engulfed in flames. Smoke alarms squealed and then stopped. A window blew out, sounding like a gunshot. He could feel the heat on his face from where he stood.

One by one, the three houses were consumed by fire, finally settling into a pile of smoldering ruins. Andy walked by Michael's post and said the radio reported that some parts of town were losing water pressure. They heard sirens wailing in the distance, but this end of town seemed deserted. They watched for the tiny smoke trails to see where hot embers fell and then doused them. Just when Michael was feeling confident, a fire started in a tall aspen tree near the gym. The water stream from the garden hoses couldn't reach that high, and as the fire began to roar through the yellow autumn leaves, the wood shingle siding on the gym began to smoke. They all ran to the spot. Andy's face sickened.

From the background of sirens one grew steadily louder, and they saw a San Francisco fire engine roar up the road, slow, and turn into the driveway. Fontaine was hanging to the back of the truck beside one of the firemen. The students shouted and pointed to the burning aspen. He jumped off and ran to the group, hugging each student and then Andy and Michael. The engine rolled across the lawn, and a fireman aimed the nozzle of the engine's water cannon at the burning aspen. Within a minute the fire was out, leaving a tree of blackened leaves dripping water. The students cheered. The firemen then watered down the smoking remains of the three houses across the street. The crackling voice on the fire company's radio sent them back down the road, but before they drove off, they attached a two-inch hose to the hydrant at the corner of the campus and showed Andy and two of the students how to turn it on.

Fontaine explained that he had driven to the building supply store out by the freeway to buy lumber for the set-building just as the fire was starting, and when he drove back toward campus the police had blocked off the streets. He drove home, got his bike, and peddled past the barricade when the police weren't looking. Several blocks from the school he flagged down a fire engine over from San Francisco and the firefighters agreed to check on the school.

One more tree caught fire, but the stream of water from the two-inch hose reached it easily. By late afternoon, the winds died down as quickly as they had come up, and the outer circle of the fire was contained. A smoky haze lolled over the school grounds. Michael borrowed Andy's phone to call Li-Li and tell her that he was okay and that the danger had passed. By early evening, the road had been opened, and several teachers and students' parents arrived. Kay Axelrod arrived, donned a yellow hardhat, and then a television news crew arrived to interview her. Michael and Andy exchanged a long glance. The last line of her interview was, "We're just thankful we were able to save the campus," Andy looked again at Michael, mouthing *we* with raised eyebrows. Michael shrugged.

Michael caught a ride back to his car in the supermarket parking lot and arrived home a little before midnight. He and Li-Li hugged tightly at the door, and Athena wagged her tail and nuzzled him with her head. When he looked into the bathroom mirror, he saw how blackened from ash and soot his face was. While he showered, Li-Li made him a bowl of noodles. As he ate, he told her all about it. She was proud of him, and one of the arrows in her heart was quivering. If he could take care of his school in a fire, he would take care of her. As for Michael, he felt a deep self-satisfaction. He had answered the call of the cow.

The school was closed for a week to allow electrical service to be restored and neighborhood cleanup to proceed. It had been dark when he left the campus on the night of the fire, so when he drove over in the daylight a few days later to get some things from his office, he was dumbstruck. Entire blocks had been reduced to charred rubble. Blackened chimneys rose from piles of gray ash, stone porches led to piles of charred timbers, and iron railings had sagged from the heat. The charred shells of cars—their make and model impossible to guess—sat on their wheel hubs, sprinkled with the ash of what had been a garage. There was an unsettling familiarity to it all, and then Michael realized why. It resembled the photographs of Hiroshima after the blast.

He drove through neighborhoods he did not recognize and for a strange, nightmarish moment felt lost. So completely altered was the landscape that he did not know where he was. Only by reading the charred street signs did he finally find his way to the school. Several hundred homes had been lost, but no one had died. Three students were among the families losing homes.

The fact that the school could have been reduced to eighteen acres of ash gave Michael pause. Just as his cancer experience had pumped new energy into his appreciation for his life itself, so did the school's surviving the firestorm deepen his sense of its value.

He knew the private school stereotype: spoiled rich kids, entitled and selfish. But in his years at the school, he could count on a few fingers the students who fit that stereotype. While most had affluent parents, the students were more soulful, humble, grateful, and caring than the stereotype.

With a school as with a nation, it is easier to sustain a culture than to change one. Michael suspected that a lot of the credit for the school culture belonged to John Johnson, who decades earlier had recruited its founding good, dedicated teachers and its first earnest, decent students. He raised money, renovated buildings, hired teachers and admitted students, all the while infusing into every classroom, stage, meeting space, and athletic field a faith that the students would be good people. He made the school into a nest where people learned, a base that made them want to be their best, a home where they found encouragement, challenge, and comfort. John was a minister—in the sense that he tended to people's needs, students and teachers alike. When he referred to "my" teachers, he meant not that they worked for him but that they were his responsibility. The winter he died was one of the rainiest on record, and one of the speakers at his memorial service suggested that the earth was weeping for him. When Jennifer spoke, she said she liked to think of them as tears that would water the earth and sustain growth for a long time to come.

In his last year, John began to allude to the time when a new head would be chosen. Michael had believed he was dropping hints about his retirement, but after John's heart attack he wondered if John had been feeling unwell and had a presentiment of his own death.

There had been a lot of worry that without him the school would suffer. But it continued to thrive. John had predicted that. "Being a head of school is like being a parent or a teacher," he has said. "You're working to bring people to a state where they won't need you any more. "

7

A month before his mother died, Michael had visited her in Indiana. She was thin and her skin looked like parchment. Though had seen her at Christmas, only six weeks earlier, the change was shocking. Still, she had not lost her zest for life, and she put Michael to work helping her get the house ready for its inevitable sale after her death. She walked briskly from room to room giving orders like a foreman (there were piles for this or that charity, piles to be sold, and a pile for the dump). Then she would have to lie down and rest for an hour, and then she would be up and active again. The hospice nurse called her amazing.

As Michael sorted through drawers and closets, childhood memories flooded his mind. Here was the fishing pole his father had taught him to use in their pond, beside it a tackle box with rusted hooks. For an instant he smelled the sour, warm pond water, then the pungent odor of the catfish he had caught and that his mother had fried for their supper. Somewhere in his memory his father stood beside him, his tanned, leathery face crinkling in a smile when six year-old Michael pulled the fish wiggling from the water. Standing in the basement closet, Michael had an impulse to put his arm around his father, to feel his father's strong hand on his shoulder. Michael thought of Odysseus in the underworld trying to hug his mother, only to have his arms pass through her ghostly image. No wonder Odysseus wept.

Here was his first baseball glove, now too small for his hand. He picked up his old wooden tennis racket, still in its press. He leafed through high school textbooks, read the "most improved" inscription on a baseball trophy. Here was his old 4-H club jacket, and there the earmuffs he wore waiting for the school bus. The flavor of the memories was the word the Greeks used, *glukupikron*. Translated as "bittersweet," it is actually *sweetbitter*, and that was the order of what Michael felt: first the sweet recall of his happy childhood, and then the bitter ache of loss.

Not an hour later, his mother assigned him to the kitchen, and he picked up and held in his hand a tiny hour glass egg timer. When it was turned over, the sands ran from one glass bulb into the other. Three minutes. He watched the brown grains rain into the bottom glass globe. They didn't make things like this any more. Timers are digital, with their LED clock faces, and time passes digit by digit, like the countdown of a space launch. No doubt they are more accurate, but the hourglass better mirrored how time seemed to pass. "Stop," he wanted to call, as if each grain represented a past moment: fishing with his father, helping his mother bake cookies, or before picking up his prom date pinning the corsage on his mother for practice.

Having lost first his father, then Elizabeth and Marilyn, and then his mother, like grains of sand falling from life, Michael sometimes felt the terror of time. He knew he would not have Li-Li forever. Eventually he would die—later if he were lucky, sooner if he were not. There was even a tiny chance that she could die first. Or she could become the dreaded shape-shifter and leave him. Sometimes when she was across from him at the dinner table, or sitting beside him on the sofa, he wanted to hit the cosmic pause button and take Li-Li in his arms and say, "Oh, Li-Li, I love you so much and I just want to hold you forever."

8

Every six months Michael had a blood test, and every one was clean. He had still not pulled a red sock from the drawer. Waiting for the results, he grew nervous, and his runaway imagination did not rest until it had conjured up a deathbed scene, Li-Li at his side, Athena whining at the foot of the bed. After receiving his test results—the lab report arrived in the mail—he felt first limp with relief, then solemn with gratitude, and finally embarrassed and sheepish at his overblown worries.

He had hoped his sexual functioning would improve over time, but it did not. Sometimes when Li-Li was out of the house, he masturbated, experimenting with ED drugs the doctor had given him. He could become only semi-erect, and he occasionally had a mild orgasm (before, if his orgasms had been a symphony reaching a crescendo, now they were the muted blare from a single trumpet).

Was this devastating for Michael? No. It was disappointing—*very*—but not devastating. He was surprised that it was not. Having come of age sexually in the post-sixties and read sex-positive authors from Anais Nin to Wilhelm Reich, he had believed that sex was central to life, foundational to one's psychology. Over the years, he had enjoyed sex with a number of women, from a couple of one-night stands to the deep physical bond he cherished with Elizabeth and especially with Marilyn. During their first summer together, he had valued his sexual bond with Li-Li. But now that he had lost sex in his life, he wondered if he had overrated its importance. Without sex, he still felt happy and whole. His *je peux* was vital.

Though he was not devastated, it was still difficult. In those first months of his relationship with Li-Li, sex had made them closer, and he missed the warmth of sex more than he missed its heat. But he missed the heat, too. When Li-Li walked through the bedroom wearing only panties and he drank in her sleek thighs and her exquisite small breasts, and when she stepped out of her panties, her pubic triangle glistening like the fur of a black she-bear, he would have given his right arm for one final lusty fuck. The problem was not just his compromised penis; he would have been happy for Li-Li to straddle his face. The first summer they were together she found his oral expertise first-rate. But Leanna had lost her desire for him, and sometimes when he desired her, a frustrated anger seethed inside him. At other times he felt sad. He doubted their sex life would be any different even if he were to recover his sexual functioning.

The worst part was realizing that in the sexual realm he was failing in his mission to make her happy. Though her sex drive had always seemed to wax and wane, she clearly had needs and desires, and he was failing to satisfy them. It made him feel terrible.

One day as he was undressing for a shower, he looked into the mirror. He wondered what Leanna saw when she looked at him. In one way she saw exactly what he saw—light struck her retina in the same way it struck his. But we do not see merely with the physical eye. We see not just red and round; we see apple and delicious—or non-delicious, for those who don't fancy applies. Objects strike us as wondrous or boring, appealing or disgusting. Chocolate mousse and cow manure are close in color but opposites on the appetizing index. Which was he to her, manure or mousse?

He certainly had known where he stood with Marilyn. She thought he was handsome, she desired him constantly, and she could hardly keep her hands off of him. There was an electric energy and a carnal wisdom in her touch. She made him feel like a handsome, appealing man. With Leanna, he felt increasingly insecure. He tried to tell himself that her lack of desire did not mean he was not desirable, but the logic provided little solace. She was the woman he loved; her eye was the only one that mattered.

Though he could—and did—live with her loss of attraction for him, he did not give up, still trying to turn things another way, still trying to author his own story. Michael had inherited from his maternal grandfather a hairy chest. During the sexual halcyon years of the post-sixties, hair—everywhere, on men and on women—had acted as a natural aphrodisiac, and women were aroused by and doted on Michael's furry chest. Sex merged with ideology: sex was natural and what was natural was sexy. Hippies had the best sex. He remembered a short-term girlfriend from when he first moved to Berkeley (she was slowly hitchhiking from Mexico to Alaska), an uninhibited girl with an all-over tan from California's nude beaches, her golden legs as hairy as his own, the hairs bleached yellow by the sun. To this day he could not think of her without feeling aroused.

But times had changed. As a photographer shooting nude models, he knew that many young women now shaved or waxed their crotches, and never did he see in a magazine a male model whose chest was not as smooth and hairless as a baby's. Li-Li had not disguised her preference for the look and feel of a hairless man, and her distaste for a hairy one. Frank claimed that many Asian women felt that way. So the next summer when Li-Li went back to Singapore for two weeks, Michael made an appointment in San Francisco to have his chest and back waxed.

The aesthetician was a nice woman of sixty who had herself been a hippie. This put him at ease. They reminisced about the days of body hair, but agreed that one had to change with the times. She explained that the wax she used was the best kind, imported from Europe. "It's going to be a little ouchy," she said. "We'll have you take deep breaths and I'll pull when you exhale."

The pain was excruciating. He grew dizzy from taking so many deep breaths. That night he shivered with hot chills on his chest and back as if suffering from severe sunburn. The next morning his chest was covered in bumps; it looked like he had taken off his shirt and rolled in poison oak. It took the bumps several days to disappear. In the mirror, he felt he was looking at a different person. Since his cancer surgery, he had been exercising more and doing more weight training at the gym, and without all the hair, he looked leaner and more chiseled than he ever had in his life. He couldn't help feeling a little proud, and he thought Li-Li would be impressed. The only flaw was a spot of sagging skin just beside his navel where one of the surgical incisions had probably severed some muscle tissue. He spent several nude tanning sessions on his deck. In the mirror he thought he saw mousse.

The first night Leanna was back, he took off his shirt at bedtime and said, a little self-consciously, "Look, I got waxed."

Leanna glanced at him and then focused on the spot below his navel where the skin sagged. "Eww," she said. "What's that?"

He explained about the surgery. Walking out of the bedroom, she said, "It looks gross."

"Well," he said to Athena the next afternoon on their walk, "I tried." He made an effort not to feel sorry for himself. As if Athena had a sense of humor, he added, "At least I don't have to suffer through getting waxed again."

And what of Li-Li? She had told Michael that her loss of passion for him was not a deal-breaker. She loved him. When they sat on the living room floor playing scrabble after dinner, Athena watching the tiles with interest, and she said, "I love our little family," she meant it. Michael listened to her better than anyone she had ever known, and even when she ranted about the same things, he never seemed bored. She knew that he loved her unconditionally. He was financially secure. His students adored him, and he made his little corner of the world a better place, and she was proud of him for that. He was competent in many areas of life—from finances to gardening–and she felt safe and taken care of by him. She admired the way he had driven to his school to fight the fire. She knew they had a good life. His care and his abiding love were the two arrows that had originally pierced her heart and bound them with silver cords. The more she heard about other husbands, the more she realized she had a good one.

And yet, seeing a hot-looking young guy in a magazine or hearing a certain song on the radio elicited from her a longing for something more exciting, something beyond all this. Her Facebook page contained links to her modeling photographs, and a couple of her college crushes who had not been interested in the pudgy chemistry nerd with glasses were now flirting openly with her through social media. *Passion* was what she wanted, and she did not feel it in her marriage. She did not desire him, and she could not remember what it felt like when she did. Sometimes she felt that by getting married she had said goodbye to a town she was not ready to leave.

There was something more. The reasons she felt proud of Michael, his qualities that made her swell with warm admiration, played like sweet sounds with a sour echo. If he was adored at his job, shouldn't she be adored at hers? If he moved with ease through his world, why did she feel insecure in hers? If Michael told her he was beautiful and that he loved her, didn't that mean that her beauty was guaranteed by his *feeling*, not by her own *being*. Sometimes she felt he caused a chemical reaction in her mind, a decomposition reaction, in which the products were the pride she felt in him but also the doubt she felt in herself. She felt inferior, and it made her angry—at him, at herself, at Life itself.

9

The following spring Michael began to teach a course of his own at San Quentin. The class was Introduction to College English, and he organized it around the theme of life stories. He assigned his students to read essays and works of fiction that told the stories of lives, and the capstone assignment was to write the story of their own lives. He savored every essay. One student wrote of being a boy in a refugee camp in Cambodia and one day walking down to the river and thinking it was full of crocodiles, only to realize they were human bodies, victims of the Khmer Rouge. A black man wrote about leaving a high school football game in Arkansas with two friends and being attacked by a gang of white supremacists; he got away but one of his friends was tied to the back of a pick-up truck and dragged to death. Not all of the stories were violent. One wrote about the tears that came to his eyes when an old man in LA showed him a certificate of slave ownership that had been passed down through his family. Another wrote about his family being known as "white trash" in his hometown; he began his essay, "When I was growing up, no one ever told me how I was supposed to be." One wrote about his personal journey from a racist skinhead to a humanistic liberal with a long pony tail. Another began his essay, "When I was sixteen, I learned I was going to be a father."

Many of the essays had errors of spelling, punctuation, grammar, and usage. A few had many. A couple had none. Michael dutifully corrected those errors in pencil. But in ink he wrote his real responses: *I admire your courage in telling this story. I am sorry this happened to you. I have faith that when you get out of here you can live the life you want to live.*

He told Leanna all about their essays. She was moved, too, and she told him that she was proud of the work he did there. One evening while the group was waiting at the outer gate, one of the teachers remarked, "Working here makes me practice gratitude. It truly does." Michael thought that she meant it made her thankful she wasn't in prison, a thought that had occurred to him as well. But he later decided that she meant that she felt gratitude to teach there, to see humans truly in repentance, and thus to participate in something so meaningful. Every day when he drove to school, San Quentin was conspicuously visible from the bridge. He always thought about his students there when he saw it, and he felt that kind of gratitude. As with every sort of gratitude he felt—for Li-Li, for Athena, for his prep-school students—it was heightened by his thanks that his cancer had not returned.

10

That summer Leanna did something that shook Michael to his core. She began participating in a Singaporean forum on the internet. Its members were female, and the topics included beauty, fashion, makeup, and celebrity gossip. Some members were also bloggers, models, or aspiring models. The forum posts had degenerated into catty snipes, cutting remarks, insults, and libel. Alliances formed. Wars raged.

Leanna—known only by a pseudonym—waded into the fray and soon became one of the most feared participants. For members who had posted photos, Leanna was a master at pointing out the flaws in their bodies and imperfections in their faces, or poking fun at bad makeup jobs or unnatural-looking hair extensions. In response to members' postings, Leanna skewered their poor writing, misspellings, or bad grammar. Leanna's posts often contained an acerbic wit that made them funny and well as mean. She felt glee in her victories.

When she revealed some of this (the least extreme parts) to Michael, he was stunned. To him, this was the worst kind of the middle school "mean girls" phenomenon being enacted by grown women under the anonymity of the internet—and one of these women was his wife! Did she have such a deep reservoir of toxic anger inside her? Remembering the cliché that morality is how people act when they think no one is looking, Michael felt ashamed of Leanna.

The forum war became Leanna's all-consuming occupation for several weeks. Her fingers raced across the keyboard of her computer as she defended by attacking. When the dust settled, she and one of her old high school friends had quarreled, and their friendship ended like a lovers' breakup. Michael suggested ways they might patch up their rift, but Leanna was uncompromising. Leanna emerged with a new friend, Samantha, one of her allies with whom she was now chatting on-line for several hours a day.

Though Michael was nonplussed, Leanna's mean side was not new to him. One evening the previous fall Michael and Leanna had been play wresting on the sofa when Li-Li complained that he had hurt her arm with a soft play pinch.

"Oh, did that hurt?" Michael asked. "I'm sorry."

A jolt of anger shot through Li-Li. "Does *this* hurt?' she responded, using both hands to pinch his arm with all her might. It left a blood-bruise that lasted a week. The physical wound troubled him less than the knowledge that she had really wanted to hurt him. He tried to imagine some circumstance in which he might want to hurt her, even for an instant, and he could not.

Michael thought about her moments of rage, her desire to run someone down on a sidewalk or to burn down the houses of his students. He found the Singaporean internet forum, and after seeing a few of Leanna's vitriolic posts, he did not want to read any more. However much she had been helped by her anti-depressant, it had not purged her of a mean streak that troubled him.

All humans are social, but not all humans are social in the same way. Some seek the intimacy of love and friendship, some seek recognition, and some seek to affect others—positively or negatively. Hitler was a people person, just not in the same way as Mother Teresa. Michael sought intimacy, the deeper the better; Leanna desired intimacy, but only in small amounts. Too much made her feel smothered and claustrophobic, trapped in a crowded house with no back door. Perhaps this explained her fantasies of fame, which we can define as love for those who don't do intimacy. Being famous is like waving from your window to people gathered in the street; you can bask in their admiration without having to invite them in.

Leanna liked to help others, but she could not resist the temptation to affect them in negative ways as well. Her *je peux* soared by flaming those models, and the psychic pain caused by an insult can be as satisfying as the welts raised by a birch switch. Let us not, out of sentimentality, deny the dark impulses that reside within us all. But Leanna had them in a larger quantity than most. They could saturate her brain like a powerful drug.

Leanna's behavior gave the snake voices in Michael's head plenty to say: she is mean, lacking in empathy, absurdly immature, and narcissistic. They were right. Michael's love for Li-Li was large, but it was not blind.

Did Leanna's behavior push Michael away? It pushed, certainly. It was as if a muscular arm placed a hand flat against his chest and gave him a hard shove. But he stood fast. His promise to stand by her always and his mission to make her happy were deeply rooted. She was the calf he would never again fail to save. The more she shoved, the stronger his determination to stay with her. She was the point of his story.

With all of the people we love—our spouse, our children, our best friends, or our parents—we have moments when we do not like them. They do something selfish or mean, annoy us with their babble, open their mouths while chewing, belch loudly. Our deeper love makes us tolerant. As Michael's love for Li-Li was great, so was his tolerance.

Here we have to ask a hard question. Was Michael's love for Li-Li paternalistic? Was there something condescending in his tolerance?

Not necessarily. There are two kinds of tolerance. One says, I am wiser, deeper, and more moral than you, and because you are less a person than I, I am cutting you some slack (which further illustrates what a good person I am). This kind of tolerance shows up in the political and social realm; sometimes one senses a deep-seated superiority in those who preach "tolerance." The subtext says, "We should tolerate those people who are less worthy than we."

The other kind of tolerance says, whatever your weakness or imperfections, I have them, too—past, present, and future—and I can imagine being in your shoes and I accept you as you are. It was the second kind of tolerance that Michael felt for Li-Li. For any mean impulse in her, he could find an echo of it in himself.

As for paternalism, there is some sense of the word in which Michael was guilty as charged. Of all the kinds of love—love of friends, love of spouse, love of country, or love of God—perhaps the most exemplary is the love parents have for their children. If we recall that oft-repeated definition of love from I Corinthians 13 (*love is patient, love is kind...*), a piece of scripture Michael had nearly memorized from hearing it at so many of the weddings he shot, no relationship comes nearer to it than the love of a parent for a child. The passage is read at weddings precisely for that reason. Love your spouse with the unselfish, deep, and abiding desire for their well-being that a parent has for its child.

Michael's patient acceptance might have surprised his colleagues who knew him as someone who did not suffer fools gladly, and a few of them resented him for it. His feelings toward Kay Axelrod had crossed the border into hatred. Kay's indifference to Anya's well-being that day of her drug overdose had so filled him with disgust that for several weeks he could barely stand to look at her face. He also felt disgusted at Li-Li's flaming of those models, but the disgust was but a polluted stream absorbed by his great ocean of love. And yet, was Kay's treatment of students as bad as Leanna's of those unsuspecting Singaporean girls? Kay was only insensitive and self-interested; Leanna could be downright mean. But Michael did not love Kay Axelrod. He had created one of those *us* and *them* divisions that plague the human race and account for civil wars, soccer riots, family feuds, and ugly divorces. Having pierced his heart three times, Li-Li was as much in the *us* camp as one can get. We are tolerant of *us*, intolerant of *them*.

Michael's tolerance for Li-Li was increased by empathy. Empathy means that, using our imagination, we put ourselves in another person's self. It is transformative, and it makes us sympathetic even to those we condemn from the outside. When Michael taught Camus' *The Stranger*, he liked to ask his students whether, if they could do so without risk to themselves, they would slip Meursault a key so he could escape. A majority of students, though fundamentally conservative and law-abiding, admitted that they would slip him a key. That is what authors do by writing in a character's point of view: they seduce us into empathy. Stories are the ultimate form of safe sex: we enter the character's body and soul. Not only do we enter Meursault's mind for all those pages, but Meursault also enters ours, and when we put down the book, he isn't easy for us to shake, even though he committed a callous, senseless, and racist murder. Our empathy for him is without moral justification and thus makes us as guilty as he. It also makes us as innocent.

This is why empathy often—but not always—accompanies love. Maybe Aristophanes, speaking in *The Symposium*, did not go far enough. Maybe our lover is not just our other half; perhaps we go beyond our own half and enter the lover. Maybe sexual intercourse symbolizes bodies not just meeting but going beyond their boundaries—or so it seems. Michael's love for Li-Li allowed him to imagine how it felt for Li-Li, as a skinny and eager twelve year-old, to be dismissed by her middle school classmates. Even if he could no longer enter her body with his body, he could still enter her soul with his imagination. Had Michael known Kay Axelrod's childhood, he might have found there some explanation of her coldness, her outbursts of temper, her desperate obsession with her resume. But we often do not want to know the stories of *them*; if we knew their stories, they might cease being *them* and become *us*.

Very likely the order in which things happen is crucial. Leanna had first pierced his heart, eventually three times, and thus he loved her and empathized with her. But what if he had seen her mean side before his heart was pierced? Perhaps that would have hardened his heart to her, and the arrows would have glanced off. He might have thought less of her than he thought of Kay Axelrod.

If love protects us against hate, so does hate protect us against love. That's why empathy with Kay Axelrod was out of the question. Michael hated her. The thought of entering her soul by means of his imagination creeped him out. Had he done so, he would have rushed home to scrub himself in the shower, gargle with mouthwash, and brush his teeth. Kay was *them*, but Li-Li was forever *us*.

11

Lysistrata is the most widely produced of Aristophanes' plays in the contemporary theater. The plot, in which Greek women conspire not to sleep with their men until the men end the Peloponnesian War, resonates with modern feminist and anti-war themes, and the satirical humor evokes from audiences a thoughtful laughter.

Fontaine always hung a large banner announcing the drama production on the front of the theater building, but this time Kay ordered Fontaine not to put up the sign—because it could attract sexual predators to the campus. "Because it's a well-know characteristic of sexual predators," Keith Bluebeard said loudly at the faculty lunch table, "that they are attracted to the Greek classics." His colleagues guffawed. Could Kay actually believe this, or did she not want Ellen's father to see the sign? He certainly knew the play was going forward. His daughter was in the cast.

Though Michael had a spotty attendance record at school drama productions, he went to see *Lysistrata*. Li-Li went with him. The modern adaptation that Fontaine had chosen was filled with risqué language, but after Kay's tirade, he had worked with some of the students to tone it down. The production went off smoothly. The cast performed well. Their sense of timing, so critical to comedy, was good. The audience found it funny and engaging, and the laughter as much as the applause marked it as a success. After the production, a smiling Kay Axelrod worked the parents in the lobby, accepting congratulations as if she had written the script. At least now Fontaine did not have to worry about his job.

Driving home, Michael and Li-Li shared in their contempt for Kay by composing a song, sung to the tune of something from the Muppets, in which the chorus was, "Kay is a hypocrite, Kay is a bitch. She'll suck your butt, as long as you're rich." When they got out of the car waving their arms and laughing, they looked at one another and cried simultaneously, "I love you."

"Collie!" they shouted in unison.

12

One day Michael was having lunch with one of his colleagues, a history teacher, and when Michael asked how she was, she laughed and said she was "hanging in there—barely." When she saw the look on Michael's face, she said, "Oh, I'm sorry. It's just that my son is a challenge."

She explained that her son, just turned thirteen, was moderately autistic, and that one of his most difficult qualities was his total lack of empathy. He lacked any sense of feeling for another person in distress or pain. While he had learned some self-control mechanisms to apply at school, at home he let out his anger, especially on his mother, and he thought nothing of saying to her, "get out of my face," or "leave me alone" or "I hate you." Michael saw in her face the pain of being constantly hurt by someone she loved.

Michael felt himself growing depressed at the conversation, and it must have showed because she laughed and said, "I'm sorry to be bringing you down."

"Oh, no," Michael said. "I just…well, I'm sorry. I can see how challenging it must be."

She had to go off to class, so Michael sat alone. The conversation had left him feeling gloomy, and he wondered why. He very much wanted to a child, but he realized that he had always assumed the child would be...well, normal. What if the child were severely autistic or had some other significant impairment? But that wasn't the pall hanging over him. Michael realized that the word *empathy* made him think of Li-Li and her lack of it.

The previous Christmas Michael had splurged and given Li-Li a Chanel clutch. It made her happy, and he could appreciate its high quality—the buttery soft leather, the exquisite craftsmanship, the elegant design. Li-Li had explored the internet to learn how to spot fake designer bags. A few weeks later she spotted one being held by a woman standing in a line at the coffee store and not very subtly photographed it with her phone, later to post the image with a nasty caption on her blog.

Leanna's lab had recently hired a new lab assistant, a young part-time Vietnamese-American student at a junior college. His name was Tran, and Leanna was relentless in her criticisms of the stupid things he said at lunch, his poor grammar when he spoke, his spelling when he wrote, his habit of talking with his mouth full of food, and the careless way he cleaned the lab equipment. She was like a shark who had smelled blood and could do nothing but attack. Everything she told Michael about the young man made it seem he was to be pitied. Did Leanna pause to wonder how it felt to be Tran, to be young and ill at ease among a group of more educated and more socially adept scientists and engineers? Or why someone might lack the money for a Chanel bag and so buy a cheap knock-off? Had she wondered, months earlier, how those young Singaporean women felt to visit their favorite forum on the web and read cutting insults about how they looked? Could Leanna lack the capacity to empathize the way some people lack an ability to sing? That thought was the dark pall that had crept over him during his conversation with Jean.

He thought of Marilyn. If anything, she had too much empathy. As a dance teacher, most of her students were female, and they recognized her as one of the teachers they could talk to. Marilyn had frequently told Michael about various students who had come to her with problems of emotionally distant parents, abusive boyfriends, eating disorders, or self-cutting. In every case, Marilyn felt their pain as if it were her own. That is the essence of empathy—if they are cut, you bleed.

Since his boyhood in Indiana, Michael had always believed in the golden rule, and in graduate school, when he was studying philosophical ethics, it drew him to Kant: Act in such as way that the rule inherent in your action is one you would want everyone to live by. Michael read deeply into Kant, and one day he found a passage that stunned him. Kant wrote that the basis for this ethics had to be grounded exclusively in reason, and he went on to say of emotion-based ethics, "such benevolence is called soft-heartedness and should not occur at all among human be-ings." To Michael this represented a division between reason and emotion that he found troubling. To him Kant was saying, act *as if* you care about someone, but don't really care. Marilyn was a person whose deepest center was filled with compassion and care.

Before the flaming incident, Michael had viewed Li-Li as having at her deepest center a soft core of goodness, and every cold, mean act, every metamorphosis into a tortoise, jackrabbit, porcupine, or tiger, was an aberration. Now he was not so sure. He still believed that at her deepest center there was a soft core of love, but along side it there seemed to reside something dark, something destructive, something hurtful and mean. Though the dark side was moderated by her antidepressants, it was still present.

The literary critic Georg Lukacs once wrote that every story answers the question, "What is the nature of man?" That's true. We noted at the beginning that in constructing a story one selects incidents, orders them, and employs poetic devices. But the storyteller always walks hand in hand with the philosopher. What is the nature of humanity? What are we here for? What does life mean? The way we tell a story reflects our answers—or our uncertainties—to these questions. Scientists sometimes talk about the "theory-ladenness of observation," meaning that even our most objective attempts to describe what is happening in the lab are shaped by our presuppositions about the experiment. The storyteller—which is to say, everyone in the world—is in the same boat. Even something as commonplace as remarking, "A leaf fell and landed on my head," is not neutral; it rests upon a pre-existing belief in the law of gravity, a sense of earthly up and down, and a calm awareness that leaves fall all the time and that they are neither sharp nor heavy. If a leaf suddenly flew up from the sidewalk and caught me on the jaw, knocking me unconscious, my presuppositions would be challenged and I would have to search for new ones.

We are not first philosophers later to become storytellers. We tell stories upon a foundation of our worldview, though sometimes the telling may induce us to alter the foundation. A soldier may return from war with a different view of human nature. Though Plato set up the poet and the philosopher as enemies, each contains a measure of the other—as so often happens with enemies!

Michael's view of Li-Li—his sense of her as a character in his story—involved one of the big questions of all time. Are humans basically good (though capable of corruption), or basically evil (though capable of acting civilly out of self-interest), or are they a contest between good and evil, their lives a tug-of-war between the two?

175

Michael's impulse had been to see Li-Li as having a center of soft goodness, sometimes led to act otherwise by her old wounds. If my mother had sent me away across the ocean when I finished eighth grade, Michael mused, perhaps I would be poking fun at my colleague for wearing shirts from J.C. Penny's.

But the fierceness of Li-Li's internet flaming threatened to burn through this philosophical foundation. Maybe deep inside her, beside that soft core of tender goodness, there lurked something else, something dark, evil, and mean. He admitted it: Li-Li could be a little shit sometimes, and she could be so because something within her was shitty.

Did this realization undermine his love for her? No, it just meant that what he was carrying against his breast was not all soft but contained thorns, and that as he loved her, so would he sometimes bleed.

13

Early that summer before the end of school and the start of Michael's summer class at San Quentin, Michael and Leanna put Athena in doggie summer camp and went to France for two weeks. One of the high points for him was the morning spent at the *Musee d'Orsay*. Michael's first memory of looking at works of art was viewing slides in his undergraduate art appreciation class. (There were no art museums in rural Indiana.) When he lived in New York, he bought a pass and went to them often. He had acquired that general sense of art history that allows one to appreciate and place in context what one is seeing. But he did not just appreciate art. He loved it.

His love of art was born of two qualities. First, he had a sensitive visual palate, and whether a fiery sunset seen from the Berkeley hills, Li-Li's sleek thighs, or Picasso's *Blue Nude*, visual beauty was one of his deepest pleasures. It was connection. To look upon beauty was to caress and be caressed.

Beyond that, he was comforted by the static quality of art. Like photography, painting—or sculpture—froze time, allowed it to be seen, studied, and held in an eternal moment. He had always had an impulse to hold on to things that moved, to hold on to time itself. Art stopped the sands in the hour glass.

When Michael was four years old, a large family-owned furniture store in his town caught fire one bitterly cold Sunday afternoon in January. Fire trucks came from neighboring towns and from rural volunteer fire departments as far away as fifty miles. Michael's father and mother bundled him up and took him to watch. Practically the whole town turned out, kept at a safe distance by the police. For a time the whole block, if not the entire downtown, was in danger. At last the firefighters got the upper hand, and only four buildings were destroyed. In the weeks afterward, even though he had been there, Michael would ask his mother or father to tell him the story of the fire—how it had started (a defective heater), how the windows blew out from the heat, how the many fire trucks filled the streets, how the firemen chopped holes in the roofs, how the fire spread to the adjoining buildings, how the water from the hoses froze in the streets so that for days to come people slipped and fell on the ice.

When he asked for the story of the fire to be told again and his father reminded him that he had heard it several times already, Michael replied, "Tell me again. Please." Years later, his parents would laugh recalling his boyhood refrain of "tell me again." Stories were like paintings in that way—they made things permanent. They rescued past events for the memory. Though literature is traditionally described as a temporal art and therefore different from painting, it is like a recorded song—one can always play it again. For Michael, stories gave him something to hold to, something to read again and again, as often as one could look at a painting. A book was like a story-telling parent, tirelessly willing to tell it again and again.

Leanna was of a different temperament. Unlike Michael, she had been exposed to art as a child. Seeing culture as a way to climb rungs on the ladder, her mother had taken Leanna and her brother to the Dallas Museum of Art. The notion of climbing rungs made an impression on Leanna, but not the art. In France she became bored with museums, impatient at how long Michael would pause and look at a single painting. Leanna liked looking at some of them, but they could be seen in a few seconds. After that, what more was there to see? That was why she liked surfing the internet. There was no speed limit, and as rapidly as she liked, she could open many windows at once, see and move on to shopping sites, gossip sites, forums, fashion, social media, games. She could set her own pace, and her preferred pace was fast.

Since Michael knew that the museums would not make Leanna so happy she could cry, he booked a reservation for lunch at Taillevent, one of the best restaurants in Paris. It was an enchanted lunch. Beginning with *gourgeres* that made Li-Li swoon—she praised their cloud-like lightness and their perfect blend of butter and cheese tastes—every course was heavenly in its taste, texture, and appearance. Sitting in a dining room with sophisticated Parisians, they savored every bite. The staff was friendly and graciously tolerant of Li-Li's mediocre and Michael's terrible French. Before they left, Li-Li charmed the maître d' into giving her a tour of the building. It made her happy and Michael's mission was in that moment fulfilled.

They took the train south, bicycling through villages, seeing castles, and one day they toured the caves at Lascaux. They both loved the tour, and Michael was struck by the simple and elemental beauty of the wall art, as if painted in the nursery school years of mankind. The painters must have had little more than a fleeting glimpse of the animals they painted (few bison will wait patiently while a man plants a spear into his side), but the paintings made them permanent, caught in midstride to be viewed by groups of tourists 17,000 years later.

Near the end of the cave tour, Michael overheard an American say to his wife that he wasn't that impressed; Michael caught the word "childish." Michael was surprised by the intensity of his own flash of anger.

Outside, Li-Li was amused by Michael's fit of rage. "*Not that impressed*—what a boorish, arrogant son of a bitch. No wonder everyone over here hates Americans."

That night at the hotel, Michael thought about the incident. He wanted to correct the man by saying "child-like," not childish. Doesn't all art emanate, in the viewer as well as the creator, from impulses that are child-like, from a basic delight in visual sensation, from the capacity to be simply mesmerized by something seen? As Michael had told Athena that afternoon on the redwood stump, he was deeply touched by Li-Li's distress at forgetting her lunch money precisely because it made her elementally human—as human as those cave painters.

The spring that Michael's mother had died, he flew back to Berkeley three days after her memorial service to resume teaching. Her death hit him harder than he had expected. One of his colleagues remarked that the death of a person's second parent leaves a void not felt after the death of the first. That made sense to Michael, for he did indeed feel orphan-like in his grief.

That spring he had a free period midmorning, and he began using it for a fifteen-minute shortcut through the redwoods to a café for a cappuccino and a muffin. The café visit and the treat were not as important as the walk over, for he developed the habit of talking aloud to his mother on these walks. The practice was even stranger because he had no belief in an afterlife. He did not believe that his words were heard by his mother or by anyone else. He did not believe that his mother, in any form other than in people's memories, existed. But still he talked to her. He would say simple things like, "I'm doing okay, Mother," Or, "I miss you Mother." Or, "Everyone at school has been very sympathetic." Or, "I got a sympathy card from old Mrs. Wallingford, my high school English teacher."

Was Michael losing his mind? He was not. He was just providing a touch of self-comfort by telling himself snippets of a fiction in which he mother's shade could hear.

In every culture, even before humans figured out how to write, there were stories. This is fact. But why? Stories—or cave paintings—do nothing to feed or clothe us, keep us warm in winter, or protect us from predators. Of course, they entertain us, but so does trying to hit a ball with a stick. Their essential function is that they provide sense to events. The animal just needs events and perceptions. Most species play. Some work. Athena did both, chasing her ball and carrying tree limbs. But a human is *homo fabricator*, a teller of stories, maker of fictions, for the fictions fill a need. These spontaneous stories in which Michael's mother listened to him were, from any sophisticated perspective, bad art, as kitchy as pulp fiction, as self-serving as a daydream, as immature as a child talking to an imaginary playmate. But its origins were in his heart, that part of the heart (from which animals are spared) that cries out, "This life must mean something."

The day after they visited the caves, Leanna and Michael rented bicycles and spent the day peddaling rural roads to charming villages. Michael began to wonder aloud how Athena was doing at doggie summer camp, where he had paid extra to have her taken on a daily hike. He voiced his worries to Li-Li. Was Athena eating well, had she become sick or been injured on one of the hikes (it was rattlesnake season), was she getting along okay with the other dogs? Li-Li then began to worry also, and she felt irritated with Michael for having brought it up.

Late that night, when it would be morning in California, he called the dog care center and was relieved to get a reassuring report. Athena was well and happy, and she had made a best friend among the boarders, a young male Lab named Buddy.

"You know," Leanna said thoughtfully to him over breakfast, "when you love something, you love really deeply." She said it with a mixture of admiration and sadness.

PART FOUR:
FOR BETTER OR FOR WORSE

1

One day Michael received an email from Marilyn inviting him to meet for lunch. He hadn't seen her in years, though soon after he married, she had heard about it and sent him a sweet note of congratulations. He felt a twinge of worry at the invitation. Could she be seriously ill? Have had a psychological relapse?

They met at a café on a day when she had a school holiday and his schedule gave him a three-hour block of free time. He had wondered why she wanted to see him, and a few minutes into the lunch it became clear that it was for closure on her part. After years of healing—and a lot of therapy—she realized how greatly she must have hurt him, and she wanted to say that she was sorry. She was dating someone, and looking down, she said, "But I know I'll never find anyone as wonderful as you."

When she looked up, both of them were blushing, and they had a tension-breaking laugh about it. She shared some information about her life (her older son had started college, she was having some lower back problems), and he told her about his cancer surgery, his dog Athena, and about teaching at San Quentin. He did not ask about the man she was dating. She did not ask about his wife. He brought her up to date on school gossip, especially the Kay Axelrod outrages. Marilyn had met Kay on a couple of occasions and instinctively distrusted her. Marilyn had good instincts in judging people.

They began to reminisce about the two years they were together, from the birthday weekend in Mendocino to her breakdown. With a good therapist, Marilyn had come to understand how reckless her first therapist had been, resurrecting the memory of her childhood trauma in a way that traumatized her further. In describing it all, Marilyn was open, honest, and introspective—as she had always been with him. They detoured around any memories of their great sex, but together they recalled a dress he had bought her, a hike around Lake Tahoe, a beach they walked at Big Sur, a yoga class they took, memorable movies they watched together. They collaborated in telling the story of their relationship. Of course, to tell a story is to relive it. As mystery stories make us lock our doors, love stories make our hearts swell. When they stood up from their two-hour lunch, they were a little bit in love again. They hugged goodbye, and he felt something electric in her embrace.

When we truly love someone, can that love ever die? Or does it lie dormant inside us, like a spring bulb in the winter ground, waiting to bloom again?

Michael shifted mental gears to teach his last class of the day, but on the drive home, he savored old memories, those they had talked about over lunch and some they had not. Not ready to return home, he pulled into the parking lot at the end of the bridge and sat on the hood of his car, staring out over the bay, thinking of Marilyn. An afternoon wind was up, and there were whitecaps on the water. He tried to calculate how long since he last saw her; it must have been six or seven years. During lunch, it felt like it had been a week. He remembered their long, lazy summer days in Berkeley, the walks around town, the sexy frolicking in bed, the empathic good will Marilyn felt toward everyone. He remembered their easy familiarity with one another's bodies. Her school was about a twenty-minute drive from his, and he remembered the time she had surprised him with a cookie left in his mailbox at school and another time when she left a love note under his windshield wiper in the parking lot. He remembered the heartfelt notes she wrote to his mother. For Michael, their relationship had created a model of what love is—a trusting and generous pledge that says, "I will let you into my heart and share with you everything that is there, and I want to enter your heart and I will accept what I find there." It occurred to him that part of the reason he was so generously loving to Li-Li was that he had learned that skill from Marilyn.

When Michael arrived home, he greeted Athena and then walked into the back yard and slumped on his redwood stump. Athena lay down, her chin across his shoe. He confronted head-on what he had been avoiding, a comparison of Marilyn and Leanna. The bald truth was that Marilyn was more loving, more giving, more physically and sexually affectionate, more adept at intimacy, and more kind. He felt unfaithful to Li-Li for allowing the thought to form, but it was undeniable that Marilyn was the better mate. That thought led to another: what if the story of Michael's life dictated that he and Marilyn should be reunited. Her shape-shifter episode now seemed like a nightmare; their reunion would be an awakening from a very bad dream. The plot arc would complete a wonderful circle. Marilyn, not Leanna, would become his Ithaka, the home to which he would return after an arduous voyage.

Athena nudged him with her muzzle; she wanted her late afternoon run. He rubbed her ears. He thought of Li-Li. She would be getting home from the lab soon. He remembered the day during their first summer together when in the heat of an argument she had thought he was about to break up with her, and she had collapsed on the floor sobbing. If parts of her felt bothered by intimacy or harbored mean impulses, there were also parts that were tender and loving. He believed in those better parts, and in precious moments he felt love emanating from her. He thought of his promise to stand by her always, first made before their marriage and later affirmed during the ceremony as a solemn vow. He thought of the letter he had written her mother promising he would always care for her. He remembered telling old Por Por the same thing in Singapore. He remembered the evening of the pomegranate cocktail and his mission to make her so happy she could cry, the first arrow to pierce his heart. He pictured her face. He thought of her decision to stay with him when he received his cancer diagnosis. He remembered those times when they said the same thing and yelled "collie." He remembered the day she forgot to bring her lunch money to work and called him at school. He thought of Li-Li weeping in her mother's arms at the Singapore airport, her mother stiff and dry-eyed in response. He thought of their first baby, Chloe or Mason.

He turned the baseball in his hand. The cover was discolored now, a dirty brown, the threads a faded red, the hard spherical shape familiar in his fingers. His story was at a junction. A momentous choice. Some philosophers would deny that, insisting that what seems choice is nothing but electro-chemical action in his brain, no more willed than the process of digestion. But brain activity is not a story. The stuff of story is the feeling of vertigo, of longing, of compassion, and of love. If Michael were not free, why did he now feel vertigo? Isn't vertigo the feeling of freedom, the realization that we coiuld choose to jump?

All the principles—his promises, his wedding vows—dictated that he stay with Li-Li, but at the moment of decision, it was not principles that swayed him; it was the picture of Li-Li's face in his mind's eye. The principles were form; Li-Li's face was content. He thought again of Marilyn, exhaled, shook his head, and said, "No." Athena looked at him and cocked her head, wondering what she should stop doing. He stepped back from the cliff. His story would be to remain Li-Li's faithful husband…as Odysseus had stayed the course on his voyage home. When he stood up, his knees felt shaky, as if he had just avoided a freeway accident. He would not call Marilyn, and he knew she would not call him. He would make a special dinner for Li-Li that night. She loved his fried chicken. He asked Athena if she were ready for her hike, and she yipped with happiness.

2

When teachers gathered for the afternoon faculty meeting, Michael noticed that three of the trustees were present. Barbara Smith, the trustee whom Jennifer and Jim went to see about Kay, was one of them. Michael was sitting next to Jim, who leaned toward him and whispered, "Do you think she's leaving?"

Kay fired up her laptop and an image appeared on the screen. There was tittering among the teachers. The image was a black and white photo of what looked like a 1930s classroom: desks with inkwells, a world globe on a stand, the teacher with a tight gray bun and a flowered dress to mid-calf, and students dressed like the cast of *Annie*. Michael noted that because the shot was backlit by the tall windows, it gave the room a gloomy, even foreboding mood. A large softbox behind the camera would make the same room look bright and cheerful. Because the image warmly reminded him of his old high school geometry teacher and her room, the tittering irritated him.

Kay raised a hand held mic and said, "That is the classroom of the twentieth century." Then she added as an aside, "It doesn't look much different from some of ours."

Smiling, Kay said, "Drumroll, please," and the faculty obliged by drumming the tables with their fingers. Pressing a key of her computer, Kay said, "And here is the classroom of the 21st century."

The new image was an architectural drawing of a contemporary classroom building, steel, glass, and concrete, set on their own campus, just above the soccer field. The slide show that followed showed six classrooms with walls of glass, high ceilings, the walls a yellow orange. Moveable walls allowed three rooms to become two or one. The chairs were plastic, the tables were wedge-shaped and on wheels. Kay's commentary, which Michael didn't follow very closely, was laced with the edu-babble he had come to hate: maker spaces, teacher as facilitator, STEM education, and collaborative learning. The architectural drawing featured pairs of students with laptops, students at workbenches, students working in groups of four. Michael did not see single slide in which he could imagine students sitting in a circle to discuss *Hamlet*.

The mic was given to Barbara Smith, who praised Kay's sense of vision. Another trustee explained that this was the first part of a grand plan to eventually rebuild the entire campus, and that this building would cost 20 million. Just after Jim whispered to Michael that they could never raise that kind of money, the mic was passed back to Kay who said they already had pledges for ten million. She was confident that construction would begin in a year. After the new building was complete, the building in which Michael now taught would be razed.

"We kept the old campus from burning down," she said, "so now it's time to use the same energy to build a new one."

3

Their house was just a few blocks from the parkland that stretched along the crest of the Berkeley hills and south into Oakland, so he took Athena on a run or a trail hike almost every day after school. She learned to find and carry tree limbs and logs—not mere sticks, which seemed beneath her—but tree limbs twelve feet long or logs that weighed five or ten pounds. She could get her mouth around a log of up to about three inches in diameter. By trial and error, she learned to find the fulcrum point of a tree limb so that she could carry it on balance, her head held high, lifting her feet in a proud trot like a Tennessee Walker. The sight never failed to elicit laughter and cheers from people on the trail. Sometimes they snapped her picture.

Michael had read about therapy dogs visiting hospitals, and he thought Athena would be a perfect candidate. He called a local organization, read through their information, and early one evening took Athena in for the test. She walked at heel through an obstacle course of people and boxes. A man opened an umbrella in her face. Someone rolled toward her in a wheel chair, another person hobbled past on crutches, and finally someone came up to Michael and began shouting and waving his arms. Through it all, Athena looked on with alert self-control. She passed with flying colors.

Their weekly gig was Thursday afternoon, two psychiatric wards at a Berkeley hospital. Athena was one of five dogs: two lap dogs, a medium-sized mixed breed, and a golden retriever. The patients on the adolescent ward were predominantly female, and most of them seemed to be there for eating disorders, cutting, or suicidal thoughts. Athena's German Shepherd *gravitas* was a magnet for the young people. The sessions were forty-five minutes, and the owners and their dogs sat in a circle on the carpet so that whoever wanted could visit.

A few of the patients ignored the dogs, remaining curled up in big chairs or sitting at a table playing cards or board games, but most seemed excited by the visits. A lot of the patients made the rounds and visited each dog. Michael made small talk while they petted Athena. Some gave her long hugs as if absorbing her calm energy. Some had dogs at home whom they missed.

The gerontology psychiatric ward was different. Here Michael and Athena walked through the day room, sitting by patients who wanted company, occasionally visiting the rooms of those who were bed ridden. Athena sensed that these people were more fragile. Once they sat next to an elderly woman whose fingers on her right hand were frozen into a tangle like the gnarled roots of an old tree, whether for physical or mental cause Michael did not know. Athena began to furiously lick the hand, as if in an attempt to heal it, and Michael gently pulled her head away. Excessive licking was against the rules.

On another occasion they sat beside a woman whose long gray hair had been done in braids. She seemed deep in a fog of dementia. Dementia patients were kept there only until they could be relocated to a long-term facility. While starting straight ahead, the woman absently began to pat Athena's head and then looked at her, as if waking up. Then she looked at Michael and spoke in a clear voice.

"Do you know Hafiz?"

Michael hesitated. "The poet? I know a little of him, but not a lot."

"Well, he has a beautiful poem about a dog. He calls the dog his beloved."

Michael told her he would try to find it. The woman looked back at Athena. A moment later she stopped petting her and resumed staring, receding into her fog. As Michael was leaving, one of the nurses told him that she was pleased to notice the woman had spoken. It had been the first time that day.

Michael thought it likely the woman's reference to Hafiz was confused, but when he returned home he found the poem on the internet. It was indeed Hafiz, a poem about a dog to whom a man bends down and whispers, calling it "Beloved." The first line of the poem read, "Start seeing everything as God."

Why do dogs keep us grounded? Because in their simplicity they remind us, if we pay attention, of what we most truly are. They want affection; we want affection. They feel lonesome or wag their tails; so do we. They have missions; we have missions. For Michael, making Li-Li so happy she could cry was his equivalent of carrying tree limbs and logs. She had pierced his heart three times, but the first—to make Li-Li so happy she could cry—was the most important because it made her the object of a mission. Four years ago, she had become the log he must carry. But "must carry" is misleading. *Must* connotes Nietzsche's camel, like Leanna's burden of the PhD program. Michael's mission was freely chosen and deeply embedded. It was a mode of self-realization, like Athena and her logs. It was his reason for living, the goal of his *je peux*, his true mission.

Every year on Leanna's birthday Michael got her a cake and presents. One of the presents was usually an activity. One year it was a hang-gliding ride from Mount Tamalpais down to Stinson

Beach (Athena watched with amazement as her mommy sailed off over the trees). Another year it was a flying lesson, and they took off from the Oakland airport in a small plane, circled the Golden Gate Bridge, and flew over the hills back to the airport, Li-Li at the controls the entire way. One year he gathered all the photos they had taken of Fungus the stuffed elephant and pasted them into a book called "The Autobiography of Fungus," complete with funny captions under each image. Whenever Li-Li was sick or depressed, he got out the book and read it to her, pausing to show her each picture. He always took her to a special birthday dinner at a great restaurant. One year, sixty days before her birthday, Michael continuously speed-dialed two telephones starting at nine in the morning, and at eleven he got through and booked a table at the world famous *French Laundry*. On that night they were given a tour of the kitchen. It made Li-Li happy.

His mission was not just relegated to her birthday. His antennae were always up for what would make her happy. She had once told Michael that her favorite symphony was Stravinsky's *The Firebird Suite*, so he watched the symphony program for two years, and when it was presented, he surprised her with tickets. In the summer they attended food festivals. He took her to as many good restaurants as he could afford. As her tastes evolved beyond midrange labels to more upscale clothes, accessories, and shoes, he took interest in them. He had bought her that black Chanel clutch she had longed for, and for Christmas he gave her a form fitting Herve Leger dress—which he dubbed a Curvy Leger dress. Because they made her happy, he encouraged her yearly trips back to Singapore. He made her happy with simple things—a flower, a favorite TV show, an offer to stop for takeout sushi. When he suggested something that she wanted, she smiled and rapidly nodded her head in a charmingly funny show of enthusiasm. He lived for these moments.

Sometimes he struck out. Once they went to a contemporary ballet performance that Michael did not like very well and that Leanna hated. Instead of saying, "this is not my cup of tea," she railed against the choreographer and the company for being terrible and fumed all the way home. At other times they would start out on a hike and Leanna would lose her desire to be there; her mood of glum withdrawal would ruin the day. Though her anti-depressants had helped the overall climate, they did not prevent episodes of bad weather. She rained on a lot of parades.

And why did not Michael call her on some of her behavior? Early in their relationship it became clear that Leanna reacted in one of two ways to any kind of criticism of her—either she responded with rage (the tiger) or she withdrew into a swamp of low self-esteem (the tortoise) so dark that she seemed suicidal. So Michael simply tolerated her moods, the sooner that they may pass. But there was also another reason. The trauma of losing first Elizabeth and then Marilyn had filled Michael with a fear it could happen again. Sometimes he felt his relationship with Li-Li was a canoe in which he was standing upright, and the danger of capsizing was great. Whenever Li-Li sensed his insecurity, it made her furious, as if he did not trust her, did not believe in her love. As a result, he tried to keep those feelings to himself.

Leanna would have said she was happy with Michael, and he would have said his mission to make her happy was succeeding. But he always felt like he was swimming against a current. The current was that Leanna was sometimes happy but often not—cranky, irritated, bored, fatigued, or just dissatisfied. When they went out to eat, when they took a road trip, when they went on a day hike, he worried like a nervous host. Would she like it? Would she be in a good mood? Would he succeed in making her happy?

4

One night Michael received a phone call at home from Fontaine. It was a Monday, and Michael had noticed that Fontaine was absent from school that day. In a quaking voice, Fontaine told Michael that the previous week he had shown a short art film containing nudity to his film class, a student's parents had complained, and on Sunday evening Kay had phoned Fontaine in a rage and told him not to set foot on campus again. On Monday she told his department head to find a permanent sub for his classes. He was being fired.

Like most private schools, this one was not unionized, and teachers signed employment-at-will contracts. In the past few years, the language of the contract had changed. When John Johnson was head, contracts stated that a faculty member could be dismissed for a "material breech" of school regulations or a "failure to abide by accepted professional standards." Now the contracts stated that employees could be fired at any time "with or without cause or advance notice." Though the administration adopted a "no comment" policy about Fontaine, in the coming days word of his firing spread, first among faculty and students, then parents, and finally alums. The school issued a one paragraph statement to the effect that Fontaine was no longer employed. Kay said there would be no further comment.

Fontaine had inspired and enlightened students for over twenty years, and alums organized a website of support. Within two weeks, over a hundred letters were posted supporting Fontaine as one of the best teachers in the school. Alums wrote eloquent testimonials about what Fontaine had meant to them. Many sent letters to the administration and the Board of Trustees. Parents rallied to his support.

The Dean of Students Deb Schmidt told various faculty members that there had been widespread student discomfort at the film, but Keith told Michael and Jennifer that there had been only one, and that the girl's hysterical parents had threatened to sue the school.

"Her father is a lawyer, so he charged that the film was a form of sexual harassment," Keith said.

Jennifer groaned. Michael rolled his eyes.

"How do you know this?" Jennifer asked.

"I can't tell you that," Keith said. "But it's definitely accurate."

Jennifer later whispered to Michael that she bet Keith was dating one of the secretaries.

"I doubt that," Michael said. "He has a girlfriend."

However Keith knew about the threatened lawsuit, the administration was weaving an alternative story. Yes, Fontaine was well liked, a testament to the loving nature of the students, but the quality of his teaching was less than his likeability, and his acts of bad judgment had become a pattern. Keith somehow also knew that Kay had taken the threat of the lawsuit to the Board and had won their backing for Fontaine's dismissal. Michael knew that if the Board was on Kay's side, their cause was lost. He felt the injustice like a burn.

A group of faculty, the old Gang of Five plus two more, requested a meeting with Kay. They met in her office. Her secretary served everyone tea or coffee in china cups. Michael declined.

In her most saccharine voice Kay cordially explained that she understood their concern, that "she loved Fontaine, too."

Jennifer and Michael exchanged looks.

"I wish I could discuss this more openly," she told them. "But because personnel matters are confidential, I really can't say any more."

Michael turned toward Kay "You think *Lysistrada* was an example of bad judgment," Michael said. "But the feedback I heard from students, faculty, and even parents was over-whelmingly positive. Every year our library puts up a display for Banned Books Week. Aren't we in danger of going over to the dark side here?"

Kay turned her frozen smile toward Michael. The occasional clink of cups and saucers was heard in the stiff silence. Jennifer repeated a similar objection. Michael, who was sitting closest to Kay, noticed a twitch in the skin under her eye. He thought she might explode. She smiled again and repeated that she couldn't answer the questions that they understandably would like to ask.

"As much as I would like to," she said, "I can't go against the advice of the school's legal council. I would love to have the luxury of debating this. I'm sure we'd have a spirited give-and-take. My first responsibility as head of school is to put the welfare of the school above all. I hope I can count on you to support me in that."

Before they had finished their tea, Kay thanked the seven for coming in and asked that they give Fontaine their emotional support in what was understandably a "trying time for him and everyone."

That weekend, Michael and Leanna sat in front of the TV to watch a DVD of the controversial film, a fifteen-minute short that had won awards at several film festivals. It featured an art student stuck in a boring nightshift supermarket job, where his fellow employees devise their own strategies to pass the hours. The student, an earnest young man, is able to freeze time and then walk through this suspended world, undress young women, draw them in beautiful charcoal sketches, and then carefully redress them, after which the flow of time resumes. During the sketching, the art student's voice-over describes his fascination with the women's beauty, not his desire for them. Michael found it an excellent depiction of an appreciation of beauty without desire, the very essence of the aesthetic. The soundtrack during the sketching scenes was Beethoven's *Moonlight Sonata*. Had the film's intent been sexual, some hard-driving piece of rock music would have been used for the score, or at least Ravel's *Bolero*. The theme of art existing outside of time mirrored exactly Michael's feelings about painting and about stories, which in their ability to "tell us again" save some piece of reality from disappearing into the past. Leanna liked the film as well, and when it was over they watched it again. The thought that the student was uncomfortable struck Li-Li as strange. "Hasn't she seen a woman's naked body?" Li-Li fumed. "Doesn't she shower after gym class? Doesn't she look in the fucking mirror?"

Kay had called the film hardcore pornography. In an email, Michael suggested to her that the film be shown to the faculty and they have a discussion of it. Kay responded that any faculty member watching the film could sue the school for sexual harassment. The reference of a lawsuit seemed to confirm that Keith was right. Michael wondered how he knew.

Deb Schmidt, the Dean of Students, and Phil Bissell, the assistant head supported Kay. Keith said, "It's either because Deb and Phil read the film as superficially as Kay did or because they swallowed their guts."

The head of a first rate college prep school was a philistine with a narrow, shallow mind, a because of it, a gifted and dedicated teacher was being fired. Michael thought he would go mad with frustration.

Michael composed a letter supporting Fontaine for the protest website, and he spent an evening wondering if he should send it. Kay was as dangerous as a rattlesnake when backed into a corner, and she might just fire him—probably not immediately, as she had fired Fontaine, but come April, she might tell him he was not being offered a contract for the coming year. There would be an uproar, but if Kay could ride out the furor over Fontaine's firing, what was one more? Li-Li encouraged him to send it. Always on the lookout for a target for her anger, Li-Li had dubbed Kay the "Botox Bitch" (Li-Li, like the women on the faculty, could detect the Kay's facial work). Michael had to dissuade Li-Li from posting a savage attack on Kay on the website. "It would make Fontaine's supporters look irrational," he told her.

Michael revised the letter a number of times to cleanse it of anger. The final version was a warm defense of Fontaine and a carefully reasoned argument against his firing. Michael wavered. Li-Li lacked Michael's realistic appreciation for the fact that he could be fired, what that would mean for his life and for their finances, how difficult it would be for a teacher who had been fired to find another teaching job. Getting fired could impact his mission to make Li-Li so happy she could cry. But Michael also had another mission—to tell the truth. Sitting at his computer, he pasted the text of his letter onto the website, hesitated, and pressed *send*.

In the coming weeks, various colleagues pulled Michael aside—into corners, vacant classrooms, empty hallways, and once into the faculty men's room with the door locked. They voiced their support for him, asked questions to see what he knew. They thought Kay's act was deplorable. But they did not send letters. They had excuses: more letters would not help and might even make things worse for Fontaine. (What could be worse that being fired? Did they think Kay would have him assassinated?) A couple suggested with an air of mystery that they could be more helpful behind the scenes.

A few teachers actually supported Kay. Fontaine's department head saw it as a chance to ingratiate herself with Kay and went on record as supporting the decision. A couple of people who had never liked Fontaine, who found him irritatingly gushy with feeling or maybe just too gay, let it be known that they were in Kay's camp. Another group, depressingly large, expressed the very dutiful opinion that after all, the job of the head was challenging, that only she knew the facts in the case, and that it was the faculty's responsibility to support her. It occurred to Michael that the McCarthy era must have been like this.

Michael had a couple of phone conversations with Fontaine. He had retained a lawyer to speak with Kay. She showed up to the meeting with both the school's lawyer and another lawyer who had been retained as a consultant. That lawyer was a member of the most notorious anti-labor firm in the city. Fontaine's lawyer had gone to the meeting hoping to appeal to reason rather than to play legal hardball. "Reason was not on the table," he later told Fontaine; he concluded that, given the school's employment contract, nothing could be done.

A retired teacher called Michael at home to ask why he had been the only one to publically stand up for Fontaine, and then she cried softly into the phone. Michael did not think himself courageous. "If I really had *cohones*," he told Li-Li, "I'd walk into Kay's office and tell her to stick my job up her ass."

After it became clear that Kay would not budge, a group of parents and alums organized an event to celebrate Fontaine's twenty years at the school. Michael was asked to speak, and he accepted. On the evening of the event, he and Li-Li drove to the rented church hall. Over three hundred people were there, including alums who had flown in from the east coast. Only half a dozen faculty attended, and Jennifer was so incensed about it that she cried.

Michael's speech began, "Enter the magician." It described Fontaine' magical powers to bring about growth, enlightenment, and self-confidence in students. Michael pulled no punches about the outrage and the injustice. He knew the speech would be posted on the internet and that Kay would see it. If they fired him for this, there might be a First Amendment angle for him to sue, and Kay would fear that. His speech captured the truth of Fontaine and what had happened to him, and the applause was thunderous. Many people wept, Li-Li among them. The speech satisfied one of Michael's missions. He had told the truth.

The next day at school, the many teachers who had not attended avoided eye contact with the few who had.

5

One Saturday that spring Michael took Jennifer's chaperoning assignment to sit with the yearbook staff while they worked laying out pages. Jennifer had come down with the flu and Kent had to coach a baseball game. Michael planned to grade essays while the students worked. Li-Li had to go to her lab to check on some experiments, so Michael brought Athena with him.

After the staff arrived, Michael took Athena out to the lawn to chase her ball, and he reminisced about the day he stood on that lawn watching the fire burn its way past the campus. The vegetation had come back, and new homes were under construction. Michael remembered how Fontaine had arrived on the back of a fire truck just as the campus was in danger of going up in flames—and how Kay had arrived later than night and gotten herself interviewed in a hard hat for the news.

He went into the yearbook advisor's office intending to grade a folder of essays, but found himself pulling old yearbooks from the shelves. He found the yearbook from his first year at the school, and though he had been almost thirty, his face looked boyish. It was strange to realize that he was at that time roughly Li-Li's age now. He wondered what it would have been like if they had been the same age and had met then. In his younger days he would not have been as dedicated to her happiness as he was now.

He looked at photos of Jennifer and Kent. Kent, too, looked boyish, and he saw something in Jennifer's face that surprised him. In her first year photograph she looked a little frightened. The fright seemed not to be a passing moment, what the camera captured in 1/400th of a second, but something deeper, barely perceptible in her face. He wondered what she might have been afraid of. It reminded him of something he had learned in his years as a photographer—we sometimes see very little of what's in front of us. We might see the store window, but not the homeless man sitting in front of it, or we might see the homeless man and his tattered, dirty clothes, but not the paperback novel in his lap. Michael wondered if in that first year he had seen Jennifer's smiling face but not the fear. Maybe it was just the anxiety that any beginning teacher feels—will I be good enough?

He thumbed other volumes and watched John Johnson's hair change from black to gray to white—but always the ebullient face, usually smiling. He looked like a man who loved what he did. Kay had a smile she could turn on, but it seemed just that—turned on. She seemed John's opposite in so many ways.

Every volume had a section on the theater and the plays Fontaine had done that year: *Midsummer Night's Dream, The House of Bernardo Alba, A Chorus Line.* Those photos, though amateurish and sometimes flawed in terms of lighting or contrast, nevertheless revealed the magic of students discovering the world of theater: the special vocabulary (blocking, striking the set), the actor's building of a new identity, the camaraderie of the green room, the magic of creating and inhabiting a world on the stage.

No longer in the mood to grade papers, he walked Athena over to his classroom, one of six in a building now slated for demolition in a couple of years. He remembered the time last winter when one of his students, walking into the room, said to no one in particular, "This room has the best vibe."

He knew what she meant. At the door the wooden threshold was worn down in the middle, polished by generations of students coming and going. The windows faced north, and during storms they rattled a little in the wind. The wooden window sills were worn smooth, varnished by years of student hands. Student desks were arranged in a circle, so every person could see with ease everyone else. One wall had a white board, and the other walls were covered in posters: The *Apollo Belvedere*, Picasso's *Guernica*, Giacometti's *Tall Walking Man*, Munch's *The Scream*, Van Gough's *Starry Night*. There were also Klimt and Matisse and a poster of the Alvin Ailey dance company. A black and white still life Michael had done hung by the door. A vase of dried lavender, a gift from Marilyn, sat on his desk, giving off just a whiff of scent.

A couple of years earlier Michael had visited a Bay Area school that resembled Kay's architectural rendering of the new building. The classrooms felt uninviting, sterile, and cold. Long tables on wheels prevented sitting in a circle. Because the walls were lined with cabinets, shelves, and pegboard, there was no place to hang art posters.

Kay had announced that the new classrooms, to be called "learning spaces," would be would be multi-use. She did not want any space that could not quickly accommodate a robotics lab, a history class, or a club meeting. To Michael, that was exactly what bothered him about the school he visited. The learning spaces had no poetry to them. They were as anonymous as a Motel 6.

Later that spring, Michael was relieved to receive a contract for the next year, though Kay included a note suggesting that if he had trouble supporting the school, perhaps he should look for another position. He resisted the temptation to write her back saying that his criticism of her *was* supporting the school.

6

Leanna grew tired of her work at the lab. She was a fast worker—sometimes at the expense of care—and she did a lot of multitasking: running several experiments at once and spending a liberal amount of personal time at her computer, checking Facebook, on-line shopping sites, even her favorite gossip blogs. In the lab she inevitably made mistakes, though probably no more than the average lab worker. Instead of pointing out to her that she had made a mistake, her supervisor, Ming, would tell her that it was her third mistake of the week, or that he couldn't understand how anyone could make such a dumb mistake, or that this was the same mistake she had made two weeks ago. She came home angry to the point of tears. Michael lent a supportive ear and comforted her as best he could. It was not easy because when Li-Li was hurt or angry she put up walls even against being comforted. The last person who had worked under Ming, a young man now assigned to a different part of the lab, had managed to laugh off Ming's scoldings. But for Leanna, Ming's berating enraged and humiliated her. She began to think of quitting.

Michael had two missions: to make Leanna so happy she could cry, and to tell the truth. What was Leanna's mission? We have said that it was to feel useful, but at the lab she felt superfluous. Leanna felt that she did not have a mission, and this distressed her. Her greatest nightmare was to feel useless, and in the throes of the depression she had suffered when they first met, she had spoken of feeling so useless that the world would be better off without her.

It would be hard for Leanna to find a mission. Missions lie before us, in the world. Things beckon to be done. There are logs to carry, truths to tell, people to be made happy. Much of Leanna's energy was directed toward herself, healing old wounds, feeling pretty, feeling full of worth, feeling high class, feeling superior. In college, she had loved chemistry and thought of the lab as a second home; chemistry had given her an identity. (She had asked not what she could do for chemistry, but what chemistry could do for her.) Michael had told her that her present work was worthwhile. The world desperately needed clean energy and her company might make a contribution to that effort. But her eyes were not focused outward. Or if they were, it was to see the world as a mirror for her own reflection.

One night when Li-Li came home for dinner, she told Michael that she had given notice that day and was quitting at the end of the week. She wanted to relax and be a housewife for a while. Michael thought her decision was impulsive. She would be eligible for unemployment—the lab would call it a layoff due to downsizing—and that would cushion the blow to their household finances and still give her money for shopping. She scheduled a month-long trip to Singapore.

Did she really want to be a housewife for a while? Probably not. She believed two things: that it was imperative to have a purpose, and she did not know what she wanted to do. Maybe she could teach chemistry. Maybe should could learn web design. She wanted to think about it in Singapore, not here.

Though Michael missed her, her emails made him feel warmed by the security of her love. He read them many times. When she did not email for a few days, he began to feel uneasy. His old fears about a shape-shifter reappeared. He had felt unsettled by her decision to leave the lab. If she had changed her view about that, what else might change? One night he read on her Facebook page (if she had time to post on Facebook, why didn't she have time to send him an email?) that she had gone out clubbing with her friend Samantha; the post gloated about the men who fell all over themselves to buy Samantha and her drinks in exchange for a few minutes of conversation.

It was raining, so he brought the baseball inside and set it on the hearth. He sat cross-legged on the floor in front of it and Athena lay down beside him.

"I mean, it's okay with me if she goes out clubbing, even if she dances with guys," he said to Athena. "But something about that post gives me the willies. It has the feeling of prostitution."

Athena looked at him with sad eyes. If a woman—or a man—bought him a drink, he would feel obliged to return the favor. It brought back memories of his disappointment when he had visited Singapore—a culture grasping and thin of soul. He began to imagine scenarios in which she met a young handsome man and fell in love. The green-eyed monster lurked in his mind.

He went to bed that night with a bad feeling.

7

Once a year the school hosted a dinner on the library patio to honor the school's most loyal supporters—meaning the biggest donors. Michael and Peggy were invited by a mother of a current senior; her husband was in Asia on a business trip and she wanted to show her appreciation to Michael and Peggy, who were her daughter's favorite teachers. Michael had taken a coat and tie to school with him, so he changed in his office and arrived unfortunately early. The library patio had been transformed. At one end a bar had been set up, tended by a woman in a white shirt and black tie. He asked for a sparkling water with lime and tried to look at ease. One of the first guests arrived, and Michael walked over and introduced himself. The man kindly told Michael that his son loved Michael's freshman English class. They chatted about his son, and at a lull in the conversation Michael asked the man what he did. He was the vice-president for marketing at a large consumer goods conglomerate.

Michael recognized the name. "Oh, yes. Detergent," Michael said.

"That's how we started. Now we're a sixty billion dollar company operating in forty countries. We have a number of subsidiaries," and he rattled off a list of well-know brand names that sounded like he was pushing his cart down the supermarket aisle.

Michael nodded. He tried to think of a follow-up question and drew a blank. He saw Peggy arrive, so he excused himself and walked over to her.

"You're like the cavalry arriving in the nick of time," he said. "I was talking to Mr. Soap Corporation and I ran out of things to say. And the conversation was only two minutes old!"

"I always feel out of my element at these things," Peggy said. "Walk to the bar with me. I think I need a glass of wine."

They surveyed the patio. Round tables for eight were covered with white table clothes and set with white china and purple napkins. Brilliant purple flower arrangements adorned each table. Purple was the school color. Their host soon arrived, and they talked with her about her daughter. Peggy was more skilled than Michael in generating praise. The catered meal was served, and the food was good, with a choice of salmon or filet mignon for the entrée. After dessert, Daddy Warbucks, slightly drunk, made some remarks and lifted his glass in a toast to the Loyal Supporters. Then he introduced Kay.

Kay smiled graciously and gave a fifteen-minute talk on the theme of the happy school. Not only were the students accomplished (she quickly rattled off their college acceptance stats, the Ivies leading her examples), but more importantly they were happy at the school. She then praised "my faculty," and added that they, too, were not just excellent teachers but happy with the school. She exuded such an earnest sincerity that Michael was dumbstruck. Could she possibly believe it? And if not, how could she speak so smoothly? Most people, when they tell a lie, often can't help tipping their hand. They hurry past the offending words, or drop their voices, or look away. Michael looked over at Peggy who gave him a quick roll of her eyes. And Kay's smile! It really was a winning smile, exuding warmth and sincerity, a practiced smile, like that of a movie star or a television weather reporter. Kay then spoke in smarmy terms of the generosity and the loyalty of the supporters being honored, and she spoke of them as those who completed the family of the school. The firing of Fontaine was the elephant in the room, so completely unacknowledged that it made Michael sad.

Driving home across the bridge, Michael thought about his abortive conversation with the soap vice-president. What had there been to talk about? No doubt there was plenty. The task of marketing dozens of products all over the world must be complex, and the successful companies had mastered it. Michael, who had realized as a wedding photographer that marketing was his weakness, should feel humbled. But at the end of the day, did it matter, in any human terms, whether they sold a million units or just a hundred thousand? Michael knew he wasn't being fair. It mattered to their employees, from truck drivers to managers. They supplied many thousands of jobs. No doubt it mattered to the company and their shareholders. Even Michael, in his modest retirement account, probably owned a few shares of that well-known company. Michael made himself admit all of that. And the man surely earned a multiple of ten what Michael earned, maybe more. But he probably did not love his job. Michael did, and he knew that such a blessing was priceless.

8

When Leanna returned to Berkeley, she told Michael that she had decided she was ready to have a baby. Michael was surprised and overjoyed. His fears about her becoming a shapeshifter had been unfounded, and he felt sheepish for having entertained them. His last great dream—to become a father—was coming true.

Now that Leanna was not working, she wanted to focus her energy on modeling again. It would be her last hurrah as a model before becoming pregnant. In the coming weeks Leanna modeled for a couple of workshops in glamour photography, a photographic genre devoted to shooting women to emphasize their beauty and sex appeal, often partially or fully nude. The work is always done in color, lit as brightly as a ketchup bottle. It has little aesthetic intent, and the images are never far from cheesecake. *Playboy* photographs are the ultimate example of glamour photography. The aspiring photographers, always men, attend the workshops like other men attend fantasy baseball spring training camps, adults indulging in games of pretend. The workshops, and private modeling gigs they produced, made Leanna feel like a star. Not just the photographers were living a fantasy; the models, too, were playing super model make-believe.

While some of the workshop models drew the line at im-plied nudes or topless, Leanna would model fully nude. Some of the lingerie she began to buy for these shoots struck Michael as more trashy than classy, but he kept his thoughts to himself. Modeling was fertile soil for the growth of her *je peux*.

Li-Li kept an on-line blog about her life as a model. She put a lot of time and energy into the website for models and photographers through which she had met Michael. She had a good sense for PR, so she commented (positively) on the work of other models and photographers, trying to build relation-ships that would result in paid shoots.

On her modeling blog, Li-Li posted outtakes from her photo shoots, reviews of make-up, and tips about diet and exercise, prefaced with the observations that she was "often asked how she maintained such a great body." She started a section called "what an off-duty model wears," and she pho-tographed the casual but carefully conceived outfits she wore to the store. Sometimes blogs soared in popularity, bringing in revenue, and she dreamed that would happen to hers. She wrote as if her audience were larger, and as if she were famous, doling out fashion advice and asking her readers to weigh in on whether she should get her hair cut shorter.

One day, when Leanna was a girl, she and her mother and brother had walked through a shopping mall near their home in Texas. They visited a shoe store having a promotion, two-for-the-price-of-one, and Ma had bought two pairs of shoes, one for Leanna and one for her brother. The sales clerk explained that the offer did not apply to one pair of girl's shoes and one pair of boy's, a restriction clearly stated in the ads, but Ma had argued until the clerk relented. After leaving the store, they walked past a dance studio, and Leanna looked through the plate glass window and saw a class of girls about her age. She recognized a girl from her school, a year ahead of her. The girl was wearing a turquoise leotard, her smooth blond hair tied in a jaunty ponytail. Ma was telling Leanna and her brother that they must always barter for a better price, but Leanna was not listening. She was looking at the girls standing at the barre in front of a mirrored wall, their toes turned outward, their knees gracefully bent, backs regally arched, one arm tracing a delicate arc over their heads. They looked so dignified, so focused, and so elegant. Leanna was mesmerized. Ma called for her to come along, but she did not move. She shifted her focus from the girls to their images in the mirror, and then she glimpsed standing in a shadow behind them a skinny Asian girl in an ugly red sweatshirt, holding a shoebox. It took an eternal second for her to recognize her own reflection.

She marched stiffly toward Ma and her brother, ripping off her sweatshirt and fighting back hot tears, ignoring Ma's warning it was too cold to take off her sweatshirt. Her brother looked at her and then looked away.

Michael did not know this story, but it would not have surprised him. Li-Li had shared memories of similar moments, and he knew she had cuts that had never healed. If a child is struck by a car and suffers a spinal cord injury or a crushed pelvis, we do not fail to see the severity of their injury. But we are less adept at recognizing wounds to the soul. It was to Michael's credit that he sensed them, and they made him love Li-Li all the more. They made him all the more desperate to make her so happy she could cry.

9

Since quitting her job, Leanna had still not found friends in Berkeley, so through the internet she chatted with old and new friends in Singapore as if they lived next door. She chatted a lot with Samantha, sometimes for several hours a day. When she was twenty, Samantha had become pregnant by her boyfriend and married him, but their marriage was now distant and strained, the husband spending money in massage parlors and Samantha having a series of affairs, often leaving the care of her young daughter to her parents. Samantha seemed not so much to have real feelings for her boyfriends as to appraise them—for their income, their possessions, how they dressed, their degree of sophistication. An attractive woman, Samantha dated one man until she found someone better; then she dumped the last one and moved on. Michael thought again of Singaporeans' "five Cs." Leanna seemed unbothered by Samantha's behavior.

Leanna asked Michael if he minded if she went to Europe for two weeks with Samantha. They would meet in Paris and spend two weeks in France and Spain.

"Instead of with me," he said in conversation with his baseball on the redwood stump. She missed girlfriend company, and he used his imagination to understand. While Michael couldn't imagine using their funds to go to Europe with one of his friends—Frank or Jack—he told himself that the continuing health of their marriage depended in part on his realizing that Li-Li was different; to ask how she would feel in his place was an invitation to failed understanding. She was not Michael; she was Li-Li, and she was different.

He told her it was okay. He went to the bank and got a hundred Euros, and the night before she left, he planted it in her suitcase with a card inviting her to treat herself and Samantha, a low budget traveler, to a nice dinner.

When Li-Li returned and told him about the shopping she had done in Paris, a second Chanel bag and a Hermes bracelet, together costing over three thousand dollars, he was stunned. He could appreciate the beauty and exquisite craftsmanship of a Chanel bag as much as anyone, and he had given her one as a present. But the second bag—and the bracelet—seemed excessive. And yet he understood the reason. She herself had once used the term "bragging rights," and that was it. The bragging rights were a balm for her childhood wounds.

She seemed pleased with her purchases, and proud and sassy when she wore them out to dinner. Any savvy marketing person knows that designer goods have an appeal beyond quality; they confer a halo of prestige on the person who owns them.

10

Michael walked toward the dining hall, lost in thought. He had just discussed with one of his classes their assignment in Faulkner's *As I Lay Dying*. He introduced a metaphor from physics. If you swing a bucket, it is the centrifugal force that pulls on the bucket and would cause it to fly across the room if you let go, but the centripetal force pulls the bucket toward its center. Planets stay in orbit because those opposing forces have found a balance. But what about families? What were the centrifugal and centripetal forces acting on the Bundren family?

As always, the students' responses, hesitant and tentative at first, built up steam and became perceptive, smart, and probing. He ended the class by suggesting that in their next journal entry they could apply this metaphor to their own families. What were the centripetal and centrifugal forces?

Michael thought of his own life. Growing up on the farm, he felt the centripetal force of love between him and his parents, his connection to everything in the house and on the farm, his friends, the adults in town who knew him by name, the stores whose owners knew him—the entire nest of warmth and familiarity. Even now, in occasional waves of nostalgia, he felt those centripetal forces pulling him back.

The centrifugal force, which began only when he entered college, was the excitement of the new discoveries he made in the wider world, from his professors and fellow students to the literature and ideas of the ages that he first found in the classroom. That was the force that guided his life since high school. His life at the school and in Berkeley, especially now that he was with Li-Li, generated a new centripetal force.

His thoughts were interrupted by sight of Jennifer and Peggy walking toward him, Jennifer with her arm around Peggy's waist as if to hold her up. Peggy's mouth was twisted and her eyes were red with tears. Michael stopped, his heart leaping against his chest. He feared something had happened to Peggy's husband. Peggy sobbed something about "all those years" and then she shrunk into Jennifer's embrace. Jennifer supplied the explanation. Kay Axelrod had called Peggy in that morning to tell her that the Latin program was being phased out.

Jennifer led Peggy between two buildings so that passing students would not see. Michael was stunned. The three began to talk at once about the idiocy and the injustice. The program was to be phased out over three years, during which time Peggy would have a part-time job. Kay had said to her, "You're probably close to retirement anyway." Peggy was sixty-five but had intended to teach for another decade.

The school's open house was approaching, and that explained the timing. The school had to make it clear that Latin would not be available to incoming students. The new view book appeared within a week, and the announcement about Latin merited a single sentence following the paragraphs about the 21st century value of the Chinese program.

A week later seven of them, the old gang of five plus Dave and Kent, met in Kent and Jennifer's living room on a Sunday afternoon. Keith named the new group the Magnificent Seven.

Michael was stunned by Peggy's appearance. She looked a decade older. It was as if all life had been drained from her face. He tried not to stare. Peggy reported in a quaking voice that her own department head called it sad but necessary, and when pressed, admitted that Kay had told her if Latin continued, budgetary constraints would mean they had to drop a Spanish or French teacher.

"Budgetary considerations!" Michael cried. "Kay makes over four hundred thousand a year. Plus the fricking car!"

"Machiavelli had nothing over on her," Keith piped in. "Divide and conquer. Set the faculty against each other."

Jennifer, forever upbeat, pointed out that the news had spread on the bush telegraph of social media, and a lot of alums who had taken Latin had phoned or emailed the school in protest. She also thought they should call a meeting of the whole faculty, something the faculty had never done on its own. They agreed on Tuesday evening in the dining hall. They all had their cell phones with them, so Jennifer brought out her faculty phone list. With scissors she cut the list into seven parts, and they all retired to different corners of the house or yard to phone their colleagues about Tuesday's meeting.

From the beginning, Michael felt he was going through the motions. His mother had been a Latin teacher, and he believed in its value. Hardly a day passed that he didn't make a reference to the Latin root of a word in his literature classes. But he saw that Kay's lock on power was secure. If she could fire Fontaine, she could do anything. Alums had rallied to Fontaine's support but were ignored. He knew it would be the same with Latin.

Within an hour, the seven reconvened and glumly reported their calls. They had reached twenty-nine faculty members and only one agreed to attend. Even the ever-cynical Keith was shocked. Some felt that Kay was merely reflecting the reality that the school was too small to support a Latin program. Others felt that Latin was dying out as a part of a liberal arts curriculum. "They don't teach Greek anymore," said one of the math teachers, "and I honestly don't see why Latin is any different." One of the department heads admitted that Kay had spoken at the department heads meeting and "made it loud and clear" that their support was essential. A few said they did not feel that a faculty meeting without the administrators was good for unity. Some said they were "uncomfortable" with the idea. A few were clearly irritated by the phone call. Her eyes welling up, Peggy excused herself, and Jennifer walked her to her car.

A couple of days later Kay sent a letter to the parents justifying the decision as part of the school becoming more future-oriented in its curriculum. She again used the quote as her own words. "We want to educate students for their future, not our past."

11

There was a four-day weekend at the end of the school quarter, and Michael splurged on a European-style boutique hotel near Yosemite. He and Li-Li took Athena with them. On the grounds of the small hotel were gardens with a koi pond, a gazebo, and a bocce ball court. Breakfasts were served on the patio in the mild autumn sun. On their first morning, they enjoyed a warm fig *calflouti* with yogurt cream, a platter of meats and cheeses, a basket of warm pastries, and freshly squeezed juices. On the second morning a fox scampered past the patio as they were eating, and the silverware jumped on the table as Athena scrambled to her feet, knocking her head on the table. After sniffing the air to her satisfaction, she lay back down. A huge bee lazily plopped onto one of the ornate spoons, seemingly drunk from the pleasure of the day. Every time they returned to the room, elves had replenished the towels and neatly arranged in aesthetically pleasing angels their personal effects, from toothbrushes on the counter to shoes on the floor. The hotel's seal had been pressed into the last square of the toilet paper roll. There were fresh cookies in the afternoon, truffles before bed, hot tea any time they desired. Li-Li was thrilled with the experience, and his mission to make her so happy she could cry was being fulfilled. His *je peux* felt strong.

They hiked a trail that wound beside a stream through the soft autumn woods. The next day they climbed a long trail and Athena swam in the cold water of the pool at the base of the falls.

On the second night they ate at the adjoining hotel restaurant, a five-course gourmet dinner celebrating the elderberry harvest. After dinner, they took a walk around the grounds with Athena, who studied the bocce ball court with keen interest and picked up one of the balls when they weren't looking.

When they returned to their room, Li-Li drew a hot bath in the large, sunken tub in the marble bathroom. She poured bath salts into the steaming water, and Michael smelled the scent of lavender wafting into the room. Through the open door, Michael watched her step out of her dress, his appreciation for her sleek thighs as acute as that day he had first photographed her. As she stepped into the tub, she called into Michael and said, "Do you want to share the bath with me?"

In that instant, three years of suppressed longing for physical intimacy surged through him, and his story promised an unexpected and long-awaited soaring to the heights.

"Really?" he called, reaching for the top button on his shirt.

"No," she laughed. "But I thought I should be polite and ask."

She intended no cruelty in her light-hearted joke. She just didn't know.

Michael lay on the bed, listening to the sloshing of her bath water. He remembered how often he and Marilyn had showered together, enjoying one another's bodies with sensual ease. As he thought about how distant he and Li-Li were in that way, it was as if a façade had just collapsed, and he was alone in an empty universe. His body felt so heavy he did not know if he could move.

When Li-Li emerged from the bathroom in a plush white robe, drying the ends of her hair wet with a thick towel, he had such a look of deathly sadness on his face that she stopped drying her hair and asked, "What's wrong?"

Only for an instant did he consider telling her.

"Nothing," he said, trying to animate his voice. "Just resting. That was a long hike today."

Satisfied, and elated from her long, luxurious bath, she made a flying leap onto the bed and kissed him on the cheek. Athena jumped on the bed with them. In his dark sadness, there was a bright light that at least Li-Li was happy, that his mission was succeeding.

Was succeeding--the verb tense was correct. His mission was ongoing. The mission to shoot a round of par golf, to get a book published, or to see Mount Fuji can succeed and then belong to history. But his mission was not to make Li-Li happy once. His mission was to make her happy continuously.

If missions are our star in the East, we still need sustenance on our journey. The incident of the bath made Michael realize how malnourished he was. In the past few years he had often longed for a hug he did not receive, yearned for sensual contact, hungered for a kiss like the first one she had ever given him, the second arrow to pierce his heart. He marched toward this mission on a frequently empty stomach.

12

Michael had brought his lunch to his classroom. While he did have essays to grade, the real reason for eating alone was to avoid his colleagues. Increasingly their decisions not to stand up—for Fontaine, for Peggy and the Latin program—disgusted him.

Jennifer walked in and laughed softly, "I knew I'd find you here. I've been eating lunch in my room, too."

"Yeah, I'm feeling a little reclusive these days."

Jennifer sat down, looked at the floor and then looked at Michael. She took a deep breath.

"I have to tell you something."

He pushed his plate to the side and looked at her.

"Kent and I are leaving. We're taken jobs at a school in Oregon. It all happened pretty fast."

"Jesus. I had no idea. I mean, I'm happy for you, but… wow."

"Kent and I haven't been feeling so good about the school. You know, Fontaine and then Peggy. Then there's the cost of living around here. And the traffic. So we started looking, and this school had openings that fit us both perfectly if you can believe that. We got interviews, then got offers. We can actually buy a house up there. It all happened in three weeks. We're still in a daze. I have to admit it, though. The catalyst was I just don't trust Kay. It has me stressed. I found out that she knows I tried to organize the meeting about Latin."

"How do you know she knows that?"

"Keith."

"Keith? Jesus. How does he know all of this stuff?"

"Well, you're going to find out more this afternoon. He's going to talk to you."

"About what?"

"He wants to tell you himself."

As they talked, Michael's attempt to show happiness for them collapsed.

Jennifer saw it. "I know," she said. "We're going to miss you, too. And I feel some guilt, like we're abandoning ship, and all that. I also feel a little sheepish that we didn't let you know, but we really didn't know how it was going to come out."

"Well, maybe Leanna and I can come up to visit you."

"We'd love that."

Michael pressed his lips in a smile.

"You know," Jennifer said, "Kent and I flew up to Oregon—the trip had to be so quick—and on the plane something slipped out of my mouth and we ended up talking about it the whole plane ride. I said that I felt like the school had been hijacked. Dangerous word to use on a plane, I know. But not hijacked by Kay alone. There's something bigger. It's in the board of trustees, the parents."

"What?"

"Just a different view of schools...and the whole world. Something corporate. That new building design. It's awful. So cold. I don't think I can explain it. But I can feel it."

After a while Michael said, "This would not be so depressing if I didn't think you are right."

Michael taught his afternoon glasses under a cloud, and soon after the last period, Keith came into Michael's room.

"Jennifer said she told you they're leaving," Keith said.

"Yes, and I'm sad to hear it. Really sad. The more it sinks in, the worse I feel."

Keith nodded. "Well, full disclosure time. I'm leaving, too."

"You, too? God, what's going on?" Michael cried.

"Okay. I need to tell you the whole story." He sat in a student desk.

Michael raised his eyebrows.

"You know I'm a computer geek. And a voyeur. That's probably part of this."

"Voyeur?"

"Kind of. So I was thinking about Kay. Back when Fontaine got the ax. She's so weird to me. It was the very next day. I was over here on a Saturday doing stuff for a new course. I know how to hack. I'm not a super expert or anything—I mean, I can't get into the Pentagon or Bank of America—but I can do the stuff that's not all that challenging. And we're all on the campus system. So I hacked Kay's email."

"Holy shit!"

"Yeah, I know. I read a lot her emails. That's all I got in to—her email account. You wouldn't believe how many emails she gets a day. Mixed in with a ton of boring stuff was some stuff that's not boring. Some weird shit. Scary shit. I can't tell you specifics, but in general, she's as bad as we think."

Michael laughed. "So that's how you always knew about everything! About Fontaine. The student's father threatening to sue and all that. Jennifer thought you had a mole. One of the secretaries."

"No. But the thing is, I got caught."

"Jesus! How?"

"By being stupid. I used my school computer. We're all in the network here at school, so our computers are not at all secure if you're in the network. I don't think people know that, but the tech department has access to our computers. It even says that somewhere, so theoretically we know it—if anybody reads those pages of small print we get every year. I don't know exactly how they made this discovery, but they found out."

"So they're firing you?"

"Officially I am"—he signaled quotation marks with his fingers—"resigning."

"Did Kay go ballistic?"

"No, and that was real weird. Ice cold, but no explosions. When I was called in, it was clear she had known about it for a couple of weeks, so there was probably an explosion I didn't see. The school lawyer was at this meeting. In fact, he did most of the talking. I was freaking out. I thought I was going to prison. Anyway, she made me an offer I couldn't refuse: I resign, and they write me a good letter of recommendation. And the school takes no legal action—they claim it's a crime. In return, I promised not to reveal anything I read. I signed an agreement under oath to that effect—it was six pages, totally lawyered—so if I ever do, they can sue me for breach of contract. They *really* emphasized that. Obviously, Kay does not want people to know some of the stuff I read. About the threat to sue me, I'm not going to call their bluff. Kay did ask me, about five times, if I had revealed anything. Naturally, I lied and told her no. But it wasn't that much of a lie, because I hadn't told much. Except I did tell Jennifer, and I'm telling you, that Kay did know we tried to call a meeting over the Latin thing. It was right after that when tech must have found out that I hacked her email and she changed her password."

"So you're looking for a job?"

"I have my first interview next week. There are lots of openings in math, so I don't think I'll have any trouble. The school is writing me a good recommendation. That's part of the deal. And my department head, who doesn't even know about this, thinks I'm just moving on. It's real clear that there's lot of stuff in Kay's emails she doesn't want anybody to know. My girlfriend thinks I had more leverage than I knew. She thinks I should have asked for big time severance pay."

Michael chuckled. "Maybe you should have."

"I'll tell you, though. This freaked me out. I was scared shitless. I'd make a terrible spy. Something about the lawyer. My mouth went so dry I could barely talk."

"Good Lord. Peggy is being phased out. Fontaine is gone. Jennifer and Kent are leaving. Now you. The Gang of Five is shrinking!" Michael raised his arms and let them drop like weights. "I feel lonesome already."

"Yeah, I feel like I'm being expelled. It's a pretty bad feeling—even though I'm kind of landing on my feet. I can't believe they wrote me a good letter."

"So what else did you find out in your emails?" Michael asked.

Keith put his hand to his mouth and made a gesture of zipping his lips closed. Then, with a serious and sorrowful look, he said, "I really can't say. I probably dodged a bullet, so I'm lying low."

13

Michael made a rough calculation of the hours per week Li-Li spent surfing the internet. During the time she was working at the lab, it was about twenty; since she had quit her job, it was well over sixty. She read gossip blogs and fashion blogs. She window shopped at dozens of clothing sites. She read posts on Facebook and played games by the hour. She read the blogs of girls in Singapore. She networked among models and photographers. He couldn't help drawing parallels to the classic workaholic (usually male, but sometimes female) who put great energy into work but had little left over for intimacy. Some of Michael's students had a parent fitting that profile. Though Li-Li's "work" was surfing the internet, her life seemed to fit the same mold.

Though Michael had made his peace with his marriage, he also wanted more.

What more did he want? He did not want to possess her. He did not want to remake her—this was no Pygmalion story. He wanted admission to her soul. He wanted to hear her thoughts, her fears, her loves, and her dreams, and he wanted her to listen to his soul in the same way. Surely he had demonstrated by now that nothing he found there would make him think less of her—he would never condemn or criticize her.

She could not lose face with him. His love was a cocoon of acceptance and abiding love. His soul was open to her in that way, and he wanted her to accept the invitation and come inside.

In spite of her resistance to such deep intimacy, Michael's commitment to her did not waver. The switch that had been flipped was still on. The arrows sent into his heart were still attached to her by their golden cords. Whatever anger, resentment, or frustrations arose, they were always washed away in a baptism of love for her. Though there were things to complain about in their marriage, he was filled with gratitude for what he did have—Li-Li, his work, and his very life. When he remembered his grandfather who had died of prostate cancer, he felt that every breath he drew was a gift from the gods.

Besides, it was Michael's mission to make Li-Li happy, to love her, not to be loved. Of course, he wanted to be loved, too—very much, in fact. But it was not his mission. We can live without the satisfaction of our wants. It is not clear that we can live without our mission.

Besides, he had a theory. He called it the tyranny of perfection. We hold out for the perfect, and in holding out, we let possibilities of real life pass us by. There was a lot he treasured about his marriage. The hug he got when he walked in the door—that was real, and it meant the world to him. Or the day when he would hold their baby. That baby would be real.

One evening Michael made good on his promise to some of his students to stay at school and watch a basketball game. As he drove over the bridge, a heavy rainstorm descended. By the time he reached Berkeley, it had turned to one of the most violent hailstorms he had ever experienced. It sounded as if a gravel truck were dumping its load on the roof of the car. Driving through Berkeley at a crawl, he saw that the hail had accumulated to the point that it looked like snow on the ground. The effect was magical. The Berkeley hills had lost power, and when he parked in front of the house, he saw a light. Li-Li had put an oil lantern on the front porch, and when he opened the door, the house was bathed in the golden glow of a dozen candles and a fire in the fireplace. Li-Li hugged him and Athena wagged her tail and nuzzled him, and he wrapped his arms around them both, feeling infused with happiness and love.

14

Having decided that she was ready to have a baby, Li-Li made an appointment with the fertility doctor. The various tests would take several weeks, and the first embryo transfer could happen as early as July. In a year, or fifteen months, or eighteen months, they would be parents of a baby, Chloe or Mason. Athena would take on a new mission as its protector. Michael would take on a new mission as a father. Like his mission to make Li-Li happy, this would be a fulfillment, not a burden. His *je peux* would soar.

This was the time that, driving home from school one afternoon, he saw the stroller rolling down Euclid Avenue and he jumped from his car to stop it. He saw it as a metaphor and a foreshadowing in his story. Of that he was sure.

PART FIVE: SILENT NIGHT

1

Hanging in the fertility doctor's waiting room was a bright blue poster showing smiling, wide-eyed cartoon babies swimming in a giant test tube. Michael liked the happy, light-hearted tone of the visual rejoinder to the questions about "test-tube" babies. Real life—and what represents real life better than a baby?—always stands up to the slings and arrows of abstract principles, be they religious, moral, or political. The sperm that had been banked in the weeks leading up to Michael's cancer surgery would be used for *in vitro* fertilization so Li-Li could become pregnant.

The IVF regimen included lots of tests and procedures for Leanna, some of them very uncomfortable. The uninsured cost was to be fifteen thousand dollars, but Michael reminded Li-Li that when the baby was born, everything they had gone through would be washed away by their joy. With interest rates low and a mortgage that was small relative to his house's value, Michael refinanced and took enough cash out to pay for the IVF and have a cushion for baby expenses. The cost did not faze Michael, but he felt guilty that Li-Li had to go through all of the medical procedures: the pelvic exams, the ultrasound, the drugs and shots, the harvesting of the eggs. Of course, the physical pain of childbearing always falls to the woman (he may have felt guilty about even that), but with IVF the burden increases. After all, he was the one whose faulty plumbing made this necessary. He told her he felt bad, and he thanked her for going through with all of it. She shrugged.

He imaged what Li-Li would look like pregnant, and he wanted to take some nice black and white shots of her at various stages. He had not photographed her for several years. She could pose in profile in front of the north-facing window in the bedroom, all indirect natural light. He would tone the prints to a creamy sepia. He would mat and frame a triptych to hang on the wall, the first shot of her pregnant, her hands folded across her belly, at five months; the second print would be same pose at eight months; and the third print would be a similar pose with her holding the baby. He could imagine the photos as vividly as if they were already hanging on the wall. He had met Li-Li by photographing her; this would bring their story full circle.

The harvesting of the eggs took place in May following a complex regimen of fertility drugs, and then they had to wait to see how many embryos were produced. The doctor's concerns about the quality of Michael's sperm caused Michael worries that he did not reveal to Li-Li. He was afraid their attempt to create a baby might end here. It was like waiting for the lab results from his blood test for cancer every six months; he wished for a good outcome so intensely that his fists clenched. A week later the doctor called with good news: they had eighteen embryos, and the embryo transplant was scheduled for early summer. He felt relieved and elated.

Now that Michael's worry about the embryos had been lifted, his longing for a child burst like the sunrise in his soul. In the past—when he was in his twenties and thirties—he would have said he wanted a child some day. But he had never wanted one like this. Every baby, toddler, and child he saw on the street, every toy store he passed, every swing set standing in a back yard became an emblem of the next chapter in his story. He imagined how attentive, careful, and protective Athena would be around the baby. He envisioned the baby on a blanket on the floor, Athena lying alertly like a lioness beside her. He so vividly imagined kissing the baby's head that his lips tingled. He felt its silky hair tickle his nose. Had he known how, he would have knitted booties.

His most vivid fantasies focused on himself and the baby. Li-Li, if she was there at all, was a vague presence, like the shadow figure in a dream. He worried how she would be as a mother, whether she would find the needed patience, whether she would be tolerant of the child's imperfections. He worried that she would become like her own mother, unloving and cold. Just as he had been the one Athena knew to poke with her muzzle in the middle of the night if she needed to go out, Michael would be a parent and a half to make up for Leanna's lower energy.

One night Michael dreamed about their baby. It was born able to talk, and Michael was having a conversation with the baby about Athena's therapy dog work at the hospital and how well the patients responded to her. The baby said that the secret was Athena's fur. "It's magic fur," the baby said. Anyone who touched it felt better. Athena was listening and understood every word. He awoke from the dream full of awe and wonder.

Michael knew that the baby's first act, upon coming into the world, would be to shoot an arrow straight into his heart. He often thought of the runaway stroller he had stopped that spring afternoon, and he savored it as a symbol in the story of his life.

Right after graduation Michael and Leanna rented a cabin for a few days on the Russian River. They swam every day with Athena, visited restaurants and small towns in the area, and read and watched television in their cabin. Athena became an efficient swimmer, and whenever a canoe passed, she glided up to it in the water, looked over the occupants, and then swam away. Sometimes she followed it for a while before swimming back to shore.

Michael imagined their trip with a child of one, or four, or seven. He imaged carrying their baby into the water, his palms under its chest and stomach, gently teaching it to swim. He mostly kept these thoughts to himself, because when he mentioned the child to Li-Li, she said little. He thought maybe she was afraid of jinxing things.

Or perhaps it was the result of going off her anti-depressants, something Li-Li had done in preparation for becoming pregnant. Though the drug was considered safe for pregnant women, neither Michael nor Leanna trusted the "considered safe." Over the years too many drugs deemed safe had later been found harmful to the fetus. Li-Li had tapered her dose, cutting back to half a tablet, then a quarter, and then none at all. As a result, she became irritable, withdrawn, and even less affectionate, as if the old tortoise, hare, porcupine, and tiger were re-emerging. She doubled her time on the couch, aimlessly surfing the internet. On many evenings, she declined to play scrabble after dinner, and when she did play, she set her laptop on the floor and surfed the internet while waiting for Michael to place his tiles. She seldom walked Athena.

One night Michael awoke to a dull scraping noise close to his head. He wondered if a mouse were under the bed—or worse, in the bed—chewing on the headboard. Michael raised himself on one elbow. Athena, lying at the foot of the bed, seemed to be awake. He could see the outline of her ears erect in the dark. The noise stopped, and then he heard it again. It was coming from Li-Li, and he realized she was grinding her teeth.

He lay on his back, wondering. He tried grinding his own teeth—yes, that was the sound. He did it again, trying to image what feeling produced it. It felt like frustration, anger. The next day he was sick with worry. At dinner that night he told her she had been grinding her teeth. She said she had done that on and off for years, and that she used to wear a mouth device when she slept to keep her from damaging her teeth.

"Is there anything bothering you just now?" Michael asked.

She rolled her eyes. "No."

Still, Michael worried about her lack of enthusiasm about the baby. She mentioned one day that when she got pregnant she would get her hair cut shorter. She had clipped a photo of the hairstyle from a magazine—crisp and efficient, but with a soft air of feminine sophistication. He took this as her acknowledgment that she was really going to be a mother. He felt that with prenatal classes and later baby groups, Li-Li would at last make some friends. Michael had female colleagues whose best friends were women they had met through baby bonding. He thought that being a mother would also make her feel useful, give her a new sense of purpose. Pushing a beautiful baby in a stroller might make her feel validated. As for the harder parts—the diapers and drool, the interrupted sleep— he would do as much of that as possible, just as he had with Athena.

When Leanna had first quit her job, she had lots of ideas for how she wanted to spend her time: she would take ballet lessons, she would learn to sew and make her own clothes, she would teach herself Mandarin. Not working promised liberation, but it had come to feel like a prison. She lacked the energy necessary to follow through on any of her ideas. One day when she went with Michael and Athena on a hike, she turned to him and said, "I think I'm having an existential crisis." She was unhappy without a job, and she wanted not to return to chemistry, but to find something new, something she could feel passionate about, something that would make a difference in the world. She thought she wanted to write, and Michael encouraged her.

"Everything of yours I've ever read has been really first-rate," he told her. He also meant it. He had seen in her writing style a real knack for a punchy cleverness.

She put together writing samples and started sending out inquiries. But being off her antidepressants darkened her sense of the future, and she was convinced she'd never find a job. Michael tried to encourage her, but to no avail.

2

The next weekend Leanna went to Los Angles for some modeling gigs. She thought of it as her last hurrah as a model. She would do a glamour photography workshop, and she also had a couple of individual shoots. Michael was teaching his summer class at San Quentin, so he couldn't go with her. On Sunday afternoon she called him to say that she was tired and wanted to stay another day.

"But the embryo transfer is tomorrow," Michael said.

"Oh, yeah. …well, I guess I'll come home today then."

He was stunned. Tomorrow would be one of the most consequential days of their lives. How could she have forgotten? He felt like the ground had slipped beneath his feet. He took Athena out for a run. As they wound their way up the trail, he wondered if Li-Li's memory lapse betrayed a deepseated desire not to get pregnant. Or was she in some kind of mental fog, the result of stopping her meds?

When she arrived home late that night, she was tired and not in the mood to talk.

She was not in the mood to talk both because she was tired but also because she did not want to reveal everything about her weekend; that is, she could tell him the events, but the story she wanted to keep to herself. That story was that she had liked the independence of traveling on her own. She hung out with an eighteen year-old model named Jade whose breast implants gave her a Barbie Doll look much sought after by glamour photographers. Leanna felt like her older sister, and she liked that feeling of maturity and greater wisdom. They had fun walking along the waterfront in Venice Beach. At her modeling gigs Li-Li felt like a star, and there was a photographer named Andre with whom she felt a spark. He was in his thirties, a car aficionado, and he did not hit on her aggressively like some photographers, but was just flirtatious enough to let her know he was attracted to her. The attraction was mutual and it made her feel alive.

We have noted that Li-Li kept a ship's chronicle, emphasizing what she did rather than what it meant. Questions of meaning made her impatient and ultimately angry. Still, every ship has a destination, however uncertain. Because she was getting no closer to a destination, she had been feeling she was in the doldrums.

We assume that missions are future-oriented. I want to do this tomorrow, or next year, or before I die—make a million, have three children, see the Grand Canyon. People compose their bucket lists. As we have noted, there is another kind of mission: the mission to change the past. Jay Gatsby's wealth— his unworn shirts, his unread library, his lonely mansion—was a means to his mission. When Nick said to him, "You can't repeat the past," Gatsby replied, "Of course you can." In fact, doing so was Gatsby's mission.

The French have a phrase, *me faire valoir:* getting myself valued. This was Li-Li's desire, the unspoken mission of her ship's pilot. Whether by becoming a famous model or wearing designer clothes, getting herself valued was an attempt rewrite the story of her childhood days when her classmates in Texas degraded her, and when her mother sent her across the ocean like an orphaned kitten. She wanted to heal old wounds by never having had them in the first place.

This is the curse of memory. Wounds may heal but scars remain. So Li-Li's posing for admiring photographers, being a big sister to Jade, and flirting with Andre were winds of *me faire valoir* blowing across the doldrums of her current life. Can we blame her for raising her sails to catch those winds? Had she been a disciple of Nietzsche, she might have proudly proclaimed she was living dangerously, as the courageous were meant to do. The weekend in Los Angeles served as an antidote to being off of her antidepressant, like a shot of strong coffee for someone sleep-deprived. It also reactivated her old fantasies of being single and in her twenties. (There was not a lot of her twenties left; her birthday was a month away and she would be thirty!) If she were single, she could move to LA, model full time, make new friends, have her own apartment and decorate it in her own way. She would be Leanna Chang, new-on-the-scene model, widely noticed, making a splash. Maybe she would fall passionately in love. Maybe she would end up being in *Playboy*. Maybe she would get herself valued.

And what of Michael, her husband? He was good to her, but he was like someone sitting beside her in a moving car. What captivated her interest, what compelled her, was what she could see through the front windshield. Did Michael deserve this? Was she being fair to him? These were questions she did not allow to enter her mind.

3

The actual embryo transfer was quick and painless, the easiest stage in the whole process. Michael was in the room with her, and after resting for a few minutes they walked back to the car. At the edge of Michael's mind, the snakes were muttering that pregnancies are supposed to begin in bed on a star-hung spring night with the smell of jasmine wafting through the open window, not in a hospital procedure room. But with the doves as allies, Michael reminded himself to beware the tyranny of pre-told stories. This was his story to tell, and in this chapter, a tiny embryo, the union of her egg and his sperm, was now inside her, and in nine months it could be their living baby. He would love their baby more than anything in the world, and as long as it was healthy, he didn't care if it were made in a toaster oven. It could also be two babies (they had implanted two embryos). Yearning, hope, and excitement swirled in his chest. His feelings for Li-Li took on a new dimension, and sometimes when he looked at her, he thought his heart would burst with love.

Of course, it was unchartered territory. Michael had spent no time in the world of scarlet-faced crying, stinky diapers, sour burping, late night fevers, and tantrums. He knew that a new baby—the great joy notwithstanding—sometimes strained a marriage. He had observed colleagues who were new parents sleepwalking through their days. But whatever he needed to know he would learn. He could do everything except breast-feed, and he was ready. He had a sabbatical coming up, and as soon as Leanna became pregnant, he would schedule his sabbatical to fall during the baby's first months. While this was a chapter in his story yet to be written, its meaning was already known: the child would be the receiver of his cow's udder of love. It would shoot an arrow into his soft catcher's mitt of a heart.

As they drove home after the embryo transfer, Leanna's thoughts were very different. She was thinking about the two embryos than had been transferred and how that meant she could have twins. Though she had previously felt that twins would be nice—"two babies with just one pregnancy," she had quipped—now she felt different. She did not want twins, and those embryos felt like uninvited guests, the doctor like the commander of an invading army.

She also was worried about the effects of pregnancy. Samantha, who struggled with her weight, wrote to Leanna in response to one of her on-line modeling photos, "just wait until you have a baby and get stretch marks." Leanna was wounded by Samantha's post precisely because she worried—a lot—about how pregnancy would affect her body. She was confident she could work out and get rid of the fat in due time (she paid close attention to models and actresses with great post-natal bodies), but stretch marks were a nightmare for her. If she got stretch marks, she was afraid she would hate the baby for causing them.

Every morning the last thing Michael did before he left the house at seven was to carefully prepare the hormone injection, then wake Leanna and administer her shot. The drug in the syringe was thick and oily, so it took longer to inject. It also required a thicker needle and the shot was therefore more painful. She complained how much it hurt, that it wasn't fair that she had to go through with this. The shots made her angry, and the fact that Michael administered them seemed fitting. It was his cancer that made this absurdity necessary. If only she had married someone like Andre, pregnancy would not mean having to wake up every morning to a painful injection. She felt like a prisoner.

While the embryos may or may not have been growing into Chloe or Mason in her womb, Leanna was flirting with Andre in LA by texting. She loved texting and she thought herself good at it; the brevity of the exchanges, the clever abbreviations, and the acronyms were conducive to fun banter. If Leanna sometimes felt at a loss in conversation, she had a quick mind for texting, and she was adept at the coy come-back, the witty rejoinder, the flirty repartee. Her texts and Andre's replies fed her hunger for *me faire valoir*. She had one more modeling trip planned in two weeks, and she reasoned that since Jade's apartment was cramped, she would accept Andre's invitation to stay with him in exchange for another modeling session.

It is not uncommon for a husband or wife, two years or six years or twelve years into a marriage, to meet someone with whom a spark is felt. It is enticing. Even in marriages where the sex is good and the attraction strong, the fresh excitement of someone new can make one feel sixteen again. Upon feeling such a spark, the spouse arrives at one of those junctions that define stories—and lives. The person can recognize the risk to the marriage and walk the other way; Michael had done this the afternoon of his lunch with Marilyn. Or the person can *carpe diem*, inflicting on the marriage a wound that may prove fatal. A third path, trying to have one's cake and eat it too, can allow the person can play the game of limited flirtation, enjoying the spark while assuming it will not start a fire. This is tough to achieve, like the dieter who, when passed a bowl of potato chips, says yes but resolves to eat just one. The game of limited flirtation is a common first step on the path to infidelity. Leanna was trying to play the game of limited flirtation.

One night, Michael had a nightmare. In the dream, Leanna told him that she did not love him and had never loved him, and he woke up screaming like a man being buried alive. Leanna called his name to wake him. She patted his shoulder and rolled over to resume her sleep. He put one arm over her and she moved away, whispering, "Go back to sleep."

He lay there for a long time before returning to sleep, and the next morning, the memory of the nightmare darkened his mood. Why do dreams have such power over us? Why does that common reassurance, "it's only a dream," fail to calm us? It is because a dream *is* a story, and while it might be a bad story, a crazy story, or an unlikely story, we cannot remain unaffected any more than we can run through rain without getting wet. Nightmares frighten us, just as erotica arouses. A dream, like a story, is a lens on life, and to dream is to look through the lens. Upon waking, we have seen what we have seen. Suppose that lens sticks to our eye, so to speak, and we began to see differently. We might, like Gregor Samsa, awake to find our life has become the nightmare, the story has become the reality. Michael tried not to look at his marriage through the lens of his nightmare.

When Leanna returned to LA two weeks later, possibly with one or two miniscule babies-to-be nesting in her womb, she had an interview at Playboy Enterprises to appear in the magazine or on the website, the result of an application she had emailed them some weeks earlier. She had not told Michael about the interview, sensing that *Playboy* fell too far short of artistic photography for his approval. Well, to hell with his approval. Though she would not be called back, on the day of her interview she told herself she might be, and it was intoxicating to walk into the building and approach the reception desk with the aura of someone who had an appointment. If the kids who had teased her in middle school could see her now! She photographed herself in front of the *Playboy* building and posted it on her Leanna the Model page. If Michael saw it, so be it.

She did another nude photo shoot with Andre (in exchange for crashing at his apartment), and the spark was palpable. Andre took her on a tour of LA and charmed her with his boyish enthusiasm for identifying all the exotic cars they saw on the streets. She saw new neighborhoods, imagined living among the rich and famous, and watched the sunset from his balcony. Her time with him felt like they were on a date.

At her photo shoots that weekend, she felt like a real model, especially at the big group shoot on Sunday. In a mansion full of models and make-up artists, photographers with top-of-the-line equipment, and large softboxes and beauty dish lights popping like muted champagne corks, it was easier to see the afternoon as an exciting day in the life of a model rather than as a gathering of paunchy, horny men who had paid six hundred dollars each to pretend they were *Playboy* photographers who might end up in bed with a model. In her own story of those days, Leanna was a professional model on the brink of something greater. Driving back from that shoot, she felt hip and young and free. She felt drunk on *me faire valoir*.

Did she think there might be the beginnings of a baby inside her? Did she think of Michael, admit to herself that even though she had not slept with Andre, flirtation was a form of infidelity? No, she avoided those elements of the story and kept her mind on the chronicle of events and how they made her feel. They made her feel good, and at this moment, that feeling trumped everything sense. What are duties in the face of an exhilaration felt in every cell of the body? While in LA, she was supposed to be religiously taking her drugs to enhance her changes of pregnancy. Did she stick to the schedule? So full of exciting activity was the weekend that she wasn't sure.

Two weeks later Li-Li received the news that her pregnancy test was negative. She called Michael at school, where he had been waiting to hear. He felt deflated but still determined. "We'll try again," he told her. "The doctor said it usually takes several tries."

For Leanna it was a sign.

4

Two days after the results of the pregnancy test, Michael took Leanna to another Michelin-starred restaurant for her thirtieth birthday, their fifth together. She seemed irritable and distracted. He told her how beautiful she looked. She thanked him. With her camera phone she took pictures of herself, alone, and she had him take a couple shots of her alone in front of the restaurant. They ordered cocktails, hers a concoction with pomegranate juice. The connection did not occur to her. Michael remembered, and as he did, a terrible thought rose in his mind like toxic smoke: he no longer made her so happy she could cry.

Driving home after dinner, he tried to tell himself that he was overreacting, as he sometimes did, and that the combination of going off her antidepressant and taking large doses of hormones for IVF was bound to affect her mood. After a while he said softly, "I love you, Li-Li." There was no answer. She had fallen asleep.

Two days later Leanna bought a plane ticket to Singapore, and she told Michael she wanted a divorce. Her explanation was the saddest cliché in the world anthology of marriage stories—though she still loved him, she was no longer in love with him. She planned to return to the states in a month and move to L.A. where she would look for a job (and presumably pursue her relationship with Andre). She told Michael that she did not want to wake up in ten years and realize that she had missed her chance for passionate love. Michael had been good *for* her and good *to* her, but now it was time for her to move on.

Her affect seemed flat and her attitude casual. The woman who had pierced his heart with three arrows had become a shape-shifter. He felt he was falling from a plane with no parachute.

On her last night in their home, she took a break from packing to have a long phone conversation with Andre. He could hear parts of it from the study where he was sitting on the floor with Athena. At one point, Leanna said, a flirty lilt in her voice, "Do you mean that if I were still a nude model, you wouldn't be my boyfriend?" It was hypothetical, of course, but also meaningful, combining fiction and reality as all flirtation does. When Michael walked into the room, she asked him for privacy, please.

She left during the first week of classes. That morning he dressed for school while she slept. Before leaving the house he crept into the bedroom and lightly kissed her on the head. She didn't stir. That day at school he felt like an animal who had been shot but not yet fallen. His mind raced. She would change her mind and be there when he returned home. She would steal Athena and take her to Singapore. She would sit down that morning and write him a heartfelt letter thanking him for being so caring during those five years. It was the promise of the letter that got him through the day. She would leave it on the kitchen table, or perhaps his desk, and its contents would serve as a life preserver to keep him from drowning. The more he thought about it, the more sure he was that this letter would be waiting for him.

The drive home had never seemed so long. Though his wildest thoughts returned (she had decided to stay, she had dognapped Athena), mostly he thought about the letter. He could see it, in her handwriting, on the table. When he unlocked the door, he was relieved to hear Athena barking on the deck. He let her in and then he checked the kitchen, then the study, the bedroom, bathroom, and living room. He checked a second time. He lifted up the pillows on the bed. There was no letter. When the phone bill arrived the next week, he saw that Li-Li had exchanged over five hundred text messages with Andre in the past three weeks, the last one as she was boarding the plane.

5

In the coming weeks Michael walked through life feeling like
an ax head of ice had lodged in his chest. He could not sleep or
eat. In the days after she left, he slept two hours one night, one
hour another night, not at all the next. After a week, he couldn't
understand how he was still on his feet. He felt distracted to the
point of danger. He lost his car keys, forgot to turn off the stove
and ruined a pan, drove the car into a curb and ruptured the tire,
and received a call from the fish market saying he had left his
wallet on the counter. One day in the produce store a little Eurasian girl looked at him, a long connected stare, and seeing her
as the child he and Li-Li would never have, Michael put down
his basket and stumbled from the store, choking on his sobs.

He called Jennifer, and she and Kent were warm and supportive. They were moving that week, but they insisted he
come for dinner, and they brought home take-out food to eat
while sitting on boxes. They tried to console him, saying the
things that people do. Two days later Michael went back and
helped them load their furniture into a rental truck.

School was in part a tonic, and it seemed that Michael's grief
stood patiently to one side for the fifty-minute periods in which
he taught his students, returning when the bell rang. Only once
or twice did during class did Li-Li or the baby enter his mind,

and a hot lump of compressed tears rose in his throat. He paused to massage his Adam's apple for a moment, and he told his students that he was battling laryngitis. As soon as his last class of the day ended, all he wanted was to return home to Athena.

He found a spa music channel on his car radio and he listened to it exclusively. When he drove across the bridge and saw whitecaps whipped up on the bay, he thought: That's how I feel. Agitated. Churning. The spa music was calming.

The first book of the year that Michael taught his seniors was *Madame Bovary,* Flaubert's masterful novel about the woman whose insatiable longing for something better, higher, and more exciting takes her through a dizzying series of infidelities, spending sprees leading to financial ruin, hobbies picked up and abandoned, periods of debilitating depression, fantasies about a glamorous life, eroticized religious raptures, and a heartless selfishness toward others, including her husband and her own little girl. He had taught the novel five or six times, and he never tired of Flaubert's masterful storytelling and picturesque descriptions. It was always interesting to see which students hated Emma and which developed some sympathy for her desire to transcend her stifling situation, only to have that sympathy tested when Emma showed herself even more shallow or selfish. It was also interesting to see which students found Charles a dullard and a chump and which students admired the fidelity of his devotion to Emma and his earnest work as a simple country doctor.

This time something was new. Michael felt he was staring into a cesspool in which the image of his own marriage was reflected in the putrid surface. How different than the expensive silks that Emma ordered on credit were Li-Li's Chanel bags or Hermes jewelry? Was Emma's indifference to her little girl—at one point she finds her ugly—so different from Li-Li's forgetting the day of her embryo transfer? When students scoffed at the naïve stupidity of Charles ("Can't he see that she doesn't love him?" they asked), Michael inwardly winced. Was he any less a chump than Charles?

Everyone knows that Flaubert said of Emma, "Madame Bovary—c'est moi." And Nietzsche said of philosophy that it is the autobiography of its author. All of us are our stories, whether we are novelists, philosophers, or just livers of our lives. But Michael's story—that his life was a journey whose end and meaning lay in Li-Li—had been upended, and now he was a man without a story. He was no longer the author of his life. His *je peux* lay scattered on the ground.

He searched for some meaning in what had happened to him. It might have been easier if in his youth he had exploited women, led them on, trampled their feelings. At least then he could believe that this was cosmic payback. But while his capacity for love and care had increased with age, he had never been a player. Li-Li's leaving him could not be redeemed by an appeal to poetic justice. Rather, it seemed to him like bad drama by a cruel storyteller, a *diabolus ex machine.*

It was not just that the plot had gone wrong, but there was a problem of character as well. Li-Li now seemed a shapeshifter. Yes, she was complex, by turns behaving as tortoise, jackrabbit, porcupine or tiger. But there was her soft center of goodness, even if it coexisted with a kernel of evil, and there was the fact that—passion or not—she had truly cared for him and loved him. How could it evaporate so rapidly? How could she have left without even saying she was sorry?

One answer was simply his own stupidity. A middle-aged man marries a younger woman. What else does he expect but that she would tire of him, look for someone younger, move on in search of herself? But to him she was not a "younger woman," and he was not "a middle-aged man." She was Li-Li, and he was Michael. Categories are sociology; individuals are story.

6

Early autumn arrived. Michael's insomnia eased, and he began to eat again. From his lean runner's frame he had lost fifteen pounds, and he began to gain back some weight. But the grief did not lessen. Li-Li occupied his thoughts almost every minute of every day, and he dreamed about her several times a night, every night. He saw a therapist who said simply, "Your grief for her is a measure of your love for her." He went to the redwood stump and sat looking at the baseball, but he could not think of a thing to say. In a fit of anger he threw it with all his might over the trees. He heard it thump against the side of a house.

One evening he took Athena to her favorite meadow as he often did after dinner. Standing in the meadow, throwing the ball for her to retrieve, he thought about the many evenings he had brought Athena this meadow. He always asked Li-Li if she wanted to come along, but she usually scrunched up her nose—how vividly he remembered that face—and said, "naw." When they had taken Athena on vacations—the scenes now replayed themselves in Michael's mind: the Russian River, Seattle, Bainbridge Island, Portland—it was always the two of them, Michael and Athena, taking long morning walks while Leanna slept and evening walks while Leanna took her shower. So it's not that different, thought Michael; it was Athena and

I then and it's Athena and I now, just the two of us. He drove back to the house feeling better than he had since Leanna left. But when he opened the door to silence, Li-Li's voice nowhere to be heard calling "Hi, Mikey," he sunk into the sofa in tears.

It had always been clear that Athena chose Michael as her primary person. Leanna had remarked on it a couple of times with a mixture of hurt and resentment. It was true. When Michael and Li-Li had been in different rooms of the house, Athena periodically checked on Li-Li, but she stayed at Michael's side. The more tangible explanation was that Michael had simply been her primary go-to person, taking her for many more hikes, taking her to the vet, taking her to Saturday morning obedience classes while Leanna slept. The other explanation was that Athena sensed he was the more faithful to the pack. Maybe Athena knew what Michael did not know— or could not admit.

Michael decided to treat himself to a massage. He thought it might help him sleep. Early in the massage he became aware of how wonderful the woman's hands felt on him, the sense of compassion and care emanating from her touch. Walking to his car in that gentle euphoria of post-massage relaxation, he tried to remember Li-Li's touch. It had been several years since she had kissed him like a woman, and their sex had been confined to the first year of their relationship. As he thought back on it, there seemed something lacking in her touch, less feeling than the masseuse being paid for a service. He remembered, too, that she was one of the few people he had ever met who did not like to receive massages—and not just from him; once on vacation he offered to treat her to a massage at a spa, but she did not want one; she took a pedicure instead.

Her sterile touch was one of the many reasons he reviewed for why she was not a great wife for him. She had betrayed him, reneged on their wedding vows, and abandoned their child promised in those embryos. She was moody, irritable, selfish, and shallow. After she had left, Jennifer told him he was better off out of it. She had a point. The snakes had been right all along, the doves naïve and clueless. But—and here is the tragic rub—he also knew in the depths of his heart, his heart three times pierced, that he had formed an abiding commitment to her that would last as long as he breathed the earth's air. The list of her faults was convincing, long, and utterly irrelevant.

Frank asked him why he wasn't more angry. His friends had choice things to say about Leanna, and his women friends were harsher than the men. The day Michael had helped Jennifer and Kent load their truck, Jennifer said, "She doesn't deserve you," her eyes welling up with tears.

He did feel waves of anger, intense anger, even moments of hatred. But he could never sustain them; inevitably they were dissolved in a bath of love.

Pondering this, Michael remembered something he hadn't thought about in years. When he moved to New York after grad school, he rented a shabby studio apartment on the Lower West Side. She took a silent vow that New York would not corrupt him into the big city indifference for which it was famous. He would not lose his Hoosier's sense of being a good neighbor.

During his second week there, Michael heard shouting in the hall one night and he opened his door to see a woman who lived on his floor, her boyfriend holding her by the wrist and slapping her while she screamed and cried. Michael shouted at the man and stepped into the hall, bracing himself for the first fistfight of his adult life. To his surprise, the man let go and ran down the stairs. Michael helped the woman to her feet. The man was her boyfriend, she explained, and he had a bad temper. She was going to break up with him. She thanked Michael profusely. He brought her glass of water and some ice cubes for her face. Two weeks later it happened again, so identical to the first time that it seemed scripted, except that this time Michael picked up a brick he had taken from his bricks-and-boards book case and left strategically beside his door. The man left again, but walking this time, and the woman again thanked Michael, but with less enthusiasm. Michael assumed she was embarrassed. The next week the scene repeated itself, but this time the couple paused in mid-fight, looked at Michael, and it was the woman who told him to mind his own fucking business.

Michael thought about the incident a lot that summer. He couldn't understand the woman's behavior, and he felt angry toward her. She must be psychologically masochistic, he thought, or just pathologically dependent on her asshole boyfriend. But now another thought occurred to Michael. Maybe the boyfriend was an essential character in her story, and she could no more abandon her story than Odysseus could abandon his. Maybe Michael was unable to hate Li-Li because she was a central character in the story of his life.

7

Michael's *je peux* was not dead. It occurred to him that he was doing better than some. He was not unable to get out of bed, he had not been drunk for a month, and he had not quit his job or lost his energy for life. If anything, he was in a constant state of agitation. He culled from self-help books on grief and divorce a list of practical things one in his situation should do, and he did them all: he ate healthy foods, exercised every day, made plans with friends and acquaintances, treated himself (massages, movies). The therapist congratulated him on his pro-active response. He found this quotation: "In depression, nothing matters, but in sadness, everything matters." By that distinction, he was not depressed but deeply sad.

He had understood that in a couple of months Leanna would return to the states to settle in L.A., look for a job, and—he assumed—pursue her relationship with Andre. For reasons he did not know, she stayed in Singapore, and she emailed him to send the rest of her things by freight. He did, and the day the boxes were picked up, it felt like the final nails being driven into the coffin.

One night he sat in his living room under the golden glow of the lamps. The only sound was the gentle rasp of Athena chewing on her bone. By a rough calculation, he guessed that he and Li-Li had spent over fifteen hundred nights together, most of them in this house. It did not seem possible. What had they done? There had been games of scrabble, rolling on the rug with Athena, conversations, snuggling on the sofa. Some nights, they had watched movies. Many nights they went into the study and he did his schoolwork while she surfed the internet. There was the night of their wedding reception when Pa raised his glass in the *Yam-Sing* toast and the night not so long ago when he returned in the hailstorm to find that Li-Li had lit the house with candles. There were the nights each December when they sat under their Christmas tree. Fifteen hundred nights—how quickly they had passed, consumed by the fires of time into the hazy smoke of memory. He wanted to reach back and grab onto those nights, make them real again, relive them, freeze them like a painting or a story, dwell in them forever.

Michael thought about their embryos. From one perspective, they were merely a group of cells, frozen in the doctor's vault. From the same perspective, the universe is nothing but energy and dust. What is life but molecules in motion? Michael had always supported the right to abortions, and he supported it still. But it was hard not to feel that in those frozen cells lay Chloe or Mason, their child who could have been.

In graduate school Michael had once heard a professor recall a scene he had witnessed while traveling in the Soviet Union. In a museum school children were being shown two large wall murals. One depicted the biological evolution of man, the Darwinian progression from one-celled life to the earliest humans. The other was a replica of the "Creation of Adam" scene from the Sistine Chapel ceiling. Though the professor did not understand Russian, he could guess well enough what the teacher was saying: the scientific view was the truth, the Biblical view a falsehood. What caught the professor's attention was the wide-eyed wonder with which the children looked at the "false" mural. Michael's professor—who of course believed in the truth of evolution, too—was making a point about the deeper truth of fiction and of art. In a similar way, Michael kept thinking of the life that could have been breathed into those embryos, and that Leanna had destroyed their children as surely as if she had strangled them in their cribs.

8

One night Michael was reading on his couch, listening to a mournful autumn rain, one hand petting Athena. He felt a hard lump in her back leg, right on the bone. Was it part of the bone? No, there was no corresponding lump on her other leg. He could not move it, so it couldn't be a cyst. Worried, the next day he took her to the vet.

The vet took an x-ray and returned a few minutes later frowning. He was pretty sure that Athena had bone cancer. How could that be? Athena seemed to feel great, and she had not been limping. It was like Michael's prostate cancer diagnosis five years earlier, a serious disease without early symptoms. After investigating canine bone cancer on the internet, Michael made an appointment at the veterinary school hospital at UC-Davis. A needle biopsy confirmed osteosarcoma. They thought Athena was a good candidate for amputation. Though Michael first balked at that option, after viewing internet videos of happy and well-adjusted tri-paws, he decided to go ahead. The chances that the cancer had begun to spread were high, but with chemo and any luck at all, Athena could get a good year. Some dogs got more.

Michael left Athena at the hospital for her surgery, and forty-eight eternal hours later, he picked her up. "It's going to be a shock when you first see her," the assistant warned. A few minutes later, she led Athena, struggling forward with a bad rolling limp, into the waiting room. Athena whimpered, and as Michael knelt and put his arms around her, she collapsed into his lap. She was shaved far beyond the incision, and a row of ugly stitches closed the skin beneath her hip. The leg was gone all the way to her torso.

For several days she did nothing but lie on her bed. Ever the good dog, she managed to limp outside to relieve herself. He fed her scrambled eggs, sauteed ground beef, and rice steamed in chicken broth. She would only eat from his hand. He had the uncanny feeling that she was trying to decide whether to go on living. After a few days, he took her walks of twenty feet, then thirty, then forty. On the fifth day after her surgery she picked up her chew-toy for the first time, and her incision seemed to be healing well. It reminded him of his own recuperation after surgery: perseverance and gradual improvement. Ten days after her surgery he took her to the meadow, and though she walked with an awkward, dipping gait, her trot was more natural, and when she ran, one hardly noticed she was missing a leg. Her fur began to grow in. She had her first chemo treatment and suffered no ill effects. It seemed her *je peux* was growing. When she got stronger, she could return to therapy dog work, maybe working wards where there were amputees.

He took a day off school to drive Athena to Davis, and he graded papers at a café for several hours while she was having her second chemo. When he picked her up, the vet had troubling news. X-rays showed some cancer in her lungs, but they hoped the chemo would halt its growth.

Though Michael still felt an aching hole in his chest left by the loss of Li-Li, much of his psychic energy had shifted to Athena. He knew Athena's days might be numbered, so he tried to drink deeply of every moment he was with her. Sometimes when he hugged her and ran his fingers through her fur, he closed his eyes and tried to feel her presence as intensely as he could. He just wanted to cling to the present moment, to stop time and forever be with his arms around his dog. It was just as he used to do with LI-Li. He thought of the film for which Fontaine had been fired and the young man who had stopped time in the supermarket so he could do his drawings. Michael wanted to stop time so he could hold his dog.

At the next chemo appointment, x-rays showed the cancer growing rapidly in the lungs, so the vet changed drugs. Michael found it hard to be optimistic. A week later, Athena began to began to lie down in the meadow as soon as she was out of the car. She stopped eating her kibble, and when he cooked ground beef, she ate it for a couple of days but then refused it, too. Michael knew the end was coming. One morning she began to stretch her neck, extending her head forward; over the phone, the vet said that indicated she was having trouble breathing. That night she woke Michael up when she jumped off the bed, walked to the door, and began to whine. Thinking she needed to relieve herself, Michael put on his coat and shoes, fastened her leash, and led her down the porch steps. She limped to the nearest bush and dove under it, burrowing into the leaves. She wouldn't respond to his call to come—something that had not happened since she was a puppy—and he had to pull her out of the bush by the collar. It was the wolf's instinct to separate itself from the pack at the end of its life, and she was blindly obeying the call of her breed. For the rest of the night she lay on the bed with her head up, stretching her neck and breathing loudly.

In the morning he called the vet and stayed home from school to await his arrival. He spread Athena's blanket by the front door. He sat with her, her head in his lap, a hot lump lodged in his throat. Outside, a cold rain began to fall. When the vet and his assistant arrived, Athena raised her head and wagged her tail once. Then she lay her head in Michael's lap. The vet used his clippers to shave a spot on her leg, and then he slipped the needle into a vein. The first syringe put her peacefully to sleep, and the second stopped her heart.

9

The days passed. Days turned into weeks, and they, too, passed. The nights grew colder, and the daylight hours shortened. It was nearly dark now when he got home from school. On nearly every block of Berkeley, something reminded him of Li-Li. There he bought her favorite cupcakes. There she liked to stop for sushi. There they had walked Athena together. Almost daily he walked past Chez Panisse, where she had stared open-mouthed at the ring on her dessert plate and he had said, "Will you marry me, Li-Li?"

The mind is a strange thing. If Li-Li were still with him, maybe three months pregnant now, his memories of her would be good memories and they would make him happy—the cupcake store, their time in Paris, their road trips with Athena, the way Li-Li crawled into the study and jumped into his lap. But now that she had left him, these very memories caused unbearable pain. Why should they not be pleasant? Because the human mind is a story-telling mind. It cannot dissociate earlier chapters from where they lead. If Odysseus had been drowned at sea, we would feel less positive about his decision to leave the cave of Kalypso. Every wonderful moment Michael had with Li-Li was now a memory, a story retelling itself, and every memory was burdened with the unbearable pain of his heartbreak. Yes, unbearable. Michael had begun to think he could not stand the void.

In a grab for his own survival, he decided to write the story of their love. Since the story he thought he knew—meeting Li-Li was the Ithaka that gave the journey of his life its meaning—was all wrong, he would try to discover the real meaning through writing. Maybe he would experience some catharsis. Hasn't that been a central function of stories through the ages? Don't we often compose stories because we are haunted by questions we can't answer, because if we don't speak, our hearts will break? Don't we tell stories because we must? Since he could no longer make her so happy she could cry, telling the truth was his sole remaining mission.

He had never written a novel, and he wasn't even sure that was what this story would be. He began, and the memories tumbled forth, filling tablets of yellow legal paper. As the tablets piled up, he imagined how some would interpret this story. Perhaps it's a feminist story, Leanna representing the problem with no name fifty years later, Michael never quite getting it and wanting her to make a baby. Maybe it's a post-feminist reversal of roles, and Michael really *was* the woman in the relationship as Li-Li had once said. Or maybe Leanna represents the psyche's ego, all self-interest, and Michael represents the love agenda of the id, lacking the intelligence of self-preservation to see that the relationship was doomed from the start. Others might see the story as a historical commentary on the immigrant in search of legitimacy through designer bags and a model's appearance. This may also imply a cultural critique, the capitalist corruption of Leanna through her consumerism and the parallel corruption of Michael's school by the power of money, Michael the traditionalist condemned to witness his own defeat. One could read this as a story of oppositional meaning systems embodied in Michael and Fontaine on one side and Leanna and Kay Axelrod on the other. Is it not also metafictional, a story about the nature of stories? Or one might suspect this story is autobiographical; the authorial voice seems to know Michael awfully well. Perhaps the reader would re-search the author on the internet and note his similarities to his character.

Or perhaps it's most deeply what the title says—love, in the form of a story.

10

Though he knew it would remind him of their Christmases past, Michael bought a tree. He found it a struggle for one person to mount it straight in its stand (Li-Li had held it while he lay on the ground and tightened the bolts), but on the third attempt he got it reasonably straight and carried it into the living room.

He wound the lights around the tree and opened the box of ornaments. Some had come from his old house in Indiana, and he remembered them from his boyhood. A couple of them had been gifts from students, some he and Marilyn had bought together, and some Li-Li had brought home from the shopping mall five years earlier. At the bottom of the box, one had broken, a large magenta ball, about a third of it gone, leaving the rest of the sphere intact and perfectly round, so that if he turned it in his hand, it didn't look broken at all. The hook was still attached to the top of the sphere, so he carefully hung it on the tree. As he did, he saw his distorted face reflected in the shiny surface, and an instant passed before he recognized the face as his own, so shocked he was by the deep sadness he saw there. It reminded him of the sad look on his mother's face the night before she died.

He sat in front of the tree and gazed at it. It was a pretty tree. Li-Li had liked their Christmas trees; she always seemed happy at Christmas, and she loved the presents he had carefully chosen. Yes, at all of their Christmases together, he had felt he was succeeding in his mission to make her happy.

On Christmas Eve Michael drove over to San Francisco for the midnight mass at Grace Cathedral. Attending midnight mass was a strange thing for a person who had not been a believer since he was a teenager, but he thought it would make a good addition to the story he was writing, and the boundary between the story he was writing and the story he was living was becoming blurred.

There was little traffic, and the drive took under thirty minutes. He parked the car on Nob Hill. In the windows of apartments he could see Christmas tree lights where people were celebrating with family and friends. How festive those gatherings must be. Grace Cathedral looked majestic lit up against the black sky. Inside, the church was nearly full. The sanctuary was bathed in golden light, and Michael took a seat in the back.

The priest began the sermon saying, "I speak to you in the name of God, the source of all being, the incarnate word, and the Holy Spirit." He spoke of how God had become a man in the form of an infant and that infants are symbols of hope. Michael thought of their Eurasian baby—Chloe or Mason—whom he had imagined so many times. If the baby Jesus was the symbol of all hope, then the embryos he and Li-Li made, once his own symbols of hope, were now symbols of his despair.

In a moment of self-reflection he thought, well, isn't this ironic, a non–believer sitting in Christmas Eve mass and feeling moved. The priest was speaking now of the Christmas story being a story about a man who told stories. And so it was. Jesus was a storyteller, a man-god who brought words to life. With Li-Li lost, the only mission remaining for Michael was to tell the truth, and that meant completing his story. His mission was now the opposite of Jesus'; instead of making the Word incarnate, he would try to render life, or a piece of it, into words.

He remembered one of the central symbols of his own story, the day the previous spring when he had stopped that runaway stroller, convinced it was a sign of the baby they would have. It seemed the story should begin with that scene.

Then the most obvious fact hit him like a brick in the face—the stroller had been empty. Had he not misread the symbol? Did not the emptiness of the stroller mean there would be no baby? If he had misread this detail, had he not misread his whole story—his whole life—as well? Not only was the baby carriage empty, but Li-Li's heart and ultimately the marriage itself were empty as well. Had he not failed to realize that living determines the story, not the other way around?

The story he had been telling had lost its goal, as if Odysseus at the end of his voyage had discovered that Penelope had forgotten him and that Ithaka had sunk into the sea.

A carol began. It was one of his favorites, "Silent Night." Though he had heard this song every Christmas season for his entire life, never had it seemed so beautifully mournful. The music rose to the ceiling of the great cathedral and then resounded, as if heaven were singing back.

"Silent Night" was first heard on Christmas Eve of 1818 in Oberndorf, Austria. After it became famous, its composer was thought to have been, at various times over two centuries, Haydn, Mozart, or Beethoven. But the lyrics were written by a young priest named Joseph Mohr and then set to guitar music by a schoolteacher-musician named Franz Gruber. While Mohr's lyrics celebrate the birth of Jesus, Gruber's melody spoke of something different. The feeling was full of sorrow, its beauty the song of a heart in mourning. Gruber's two young children had died by then, and though his intent was to compose music for Mohr's Christmas lyrics about the birth of a child and the hope it promised, the result was a song of mourning, an expression of grief over the death of his two children.

With the rest of the congregation, Michael stood. With the music as background, so peaceful and sad, he cocked his head as if hearing in the carol the scene that would end his own story.

Yes. That was it. The service would end, and in his story he would leave the candlelight for the cold night air and the silver light of the half moon. Walking to his car, he would see Christmas tree lights still glowing in living room windows. He would drive down Lombard Street and take the last exit before the bridge, drive into the lot and park his car, leaving the keys on the driver's seat.

Nietzsche wrote, "Die at the right time."

Sometimes stories reach a point at which they must end.

With the will of a character determined by his story and enacting his assigned role, he would walk out onto the bridge. Looking to the east, he would see the winking lights of the Berkeley hills where he had lived with Li-Li in dedication and love. He would hear the occasional whoosh of tires as he walked rapidly along the sidewalk on the bridge. Looking left, toward the Pacific, he would see only darkness. Thousands of miles in that direction lay the city-nation of Singapore where it would be late Christmas afternoon already. For the past three months he had always known the hour in Singapore, California time plus fifteen hours. Li-Li might have thought of him, briefly, and some memory from their five Christmases together might have entered the chronicle of her mind. Michael would walk briskly, and when he reached mid-span, without hesitation he would put his hands on the four-foot railing, climb over, turn his body around, and let go.

The surface of the water lies 220 feet below and the fall lasts four seconds, enough time for a complete thought, pregnant with meaning, a final sentence in his story. The sensation of the plunging fall and the sound—that rushing wind noise—would remind him of their skydive from the plane, and in his last thought he would remember his words to his tandem instructor after the chute opened, the words he could not recall that day but remembered now. Floating in peaceful silence, he had looked skyward and asked, "Where's Li-Li?"

Acknowledgements

Though writing is solitary, it draws upon a lifetime of blessings—and curses. Among my valuable blessings have been two loving parents, some great teachers from kindergarten to graduate school, writers whose works I have treasured, generations of students who have been my *raison d'être*, and some real friends, three of whom (Fadge, Jack, and Nabs) generously read an early version of this book.

About the Author

Bill Smoot grew up in Maysville, Kentucky. His life as a writer began at age sixteen when, following an announcement at school that President Kennedy had been shot, he heard a classmate say, "I hope he dies." In response he wrote an opinion piece for the school paper, and from that point he took up the pen as a kind of sword, trying to fight, in his modest way, for things humane and things true.

He received his BA from Purdue University where he was editor of the student newspaper, *The Exponent.* In his editorials and columns he weighed in on the issues of the day. In response, the university president tried to fire him as editor and was forced to back down when the campus rose up in protest.

Mr. Smoot received his PhD in philosophy from Northwestern University and taught at Miami University in Ohio. He moved to California where he taught in private schools for four decades. His essays and short fiction have appeared in a number of publications, among them *The Nation, Literary Review, Crab Orchard Review, Orchid, Tupelo Quarterly*, and *Salon.com*. He is also the author of *Conversations with Great Teachers,* a book of interviews with great teachers from across the country. He has been a fine art photographer specializing in black and white. He currently teaches OLLI courses at

UC-Berkeley and with the Prison University Project at San Quentin Prison. He lives in Berkeley with his dog Artemis.

Made in the USA
San Bernardino,
CA